Praise for *Enchanted Air*

A Pura Belpré Author Award winner

A Walter Honor Book

Finalist, YALSA Award for Excellence in Nonfiction

An Arnold Adoff Teen Poetry Award winner

★"We need more of these stories, especially when they are as beautifully told as this one."—*Kirkus Reviews*, starred review

★"Any child who has felt like an outsider will recognize themselves in Margarita's tale."—*School Library Journal*, starred review

★"Engle's memoir in verse is, indeed, nothing short of enchanting. . . . The book's poignancy and layered beauty make it a worthy addition to any collection."—*Booklist*, starred review

Praise for *Lion Island*

★"A beautifully written, thought-provoking work from a highly regarded author and poet."—*School Library Journal*, starred review

"Tenderly exposes the rage and hope that can exist within the same heart. A fierce portrait of a young man's discovery of power through words."—*Kirkus Reviews*

"Engle's characters speak eloquently about gender inequality, racial injustice, and becoming a 'warrior of words' through diplomatic and written means."—*Publishers Weekly*

Verse Novels by
MARGARITA ENGLE

SOARING EARTH:
A Companion Memoir to Enchanted Air

JAZZ OWLS:
A Novel of the Zoot Suit Riots

LION ISLAND:
Cuba's Warrior of Words

ENCHANTED AIR:
Two Cultures, Two Wings: A Memoir

SILVER PEOPLE:
Voices from the Panama Canal

THE LIGHTNING DREAMER:
Cuba's Greatest Abolitionist

THE WILD BOOK

HURRICANE DANCERS:
The First Caribbean Pirate Shipwreck

THE FIREFLY LETTERS:
A Suffragette's Journey to Cuba

TROPICAL SECRETS:
Holocaust Refugees in Cuba

THE SURRENDER TREE:
Poems of Cuba's Struggle for Freedom

THE POET SLAVE OF CUBA:
A Biography of Juan Francisco Manzano

FOREST WORLD

MARGARITA ENGLE

ATHENEUM BOOKS FOR YOUNG READERS
New York London Toronto Sydney New Delhi

atheneum

ATHENEUM BOOKS FOR YOUNG READERS
An imprint of Simon & Schuster Children's Publishing Division
1230 Avenue of the Americas, New York, New York 10020
This book is a work of fiction. Any references to historical events, real people, or real places are used fictitiously. Other names, characters, places, and events are products of the author's imagination, and any resemblance to actual events or places or persons, living or dead, is entirely coincidental.
Text copyright © 2017 by Margarita Engle
Cover and title page illustrations copyright © 2017 by Joe Cepeda
All rights reserved, including the right of reproduction in whole or in part in any form.
ATHENEUM BOOKS FOR YOUNG READERS is a registered trademark of Simon & Schuster, Inc.
Atheneum logo is a trademark of Simon & Schuster, Inc.
For information about special discounts for bulk purchases, please contact Simon & Schuster Special Sales at 1-866-506-1949 or business@simonandschuster.com.
The Simon & Schuster Speakers Bureau can bring authors to your live event. For more information or to book an event, contact the Simon & Schuster Speakers Bureau at 1-866-248-3049 or visit our website at www.simonspeakers.com.
Also available in an Atheneum Books for Young Readers hardcover edition
Book design by Sonia Chaghatzbanian and Irene Metaxatos
The text for this book was set in Simoncini Garamond Std.
Manufactured in the United States of America
0519 OFF
First Atheneum Books for Young Readers paperback edition August 2018
10 9 8 7 6 5 4 3 2
The Library of Congress has cataloged the hardcover edition as follows:
Names: Engle, Margarita, author.
Title: Forest world / Margarita Engle.
Description: First edition. | New York : Atheneum, [2017] | Summary: Sent to Cuba to visit the father he barely knows, Edver is surprised to meet a half-sister, Luza, whose plan to lure their cryptozoologist mother into coming there, too, turns dangerous. | Includes bibliographical references.
Identifiers: LCCN 2016046561
Subjects: | CYAC: Novels in verse. | Brothers and sisters—Fiction. | Family life—Cuba—Fiction. | Forests and forestry—Fiction. | Poaching—Fiction. | Cuba—Fiction. | BISAC: JUVENILE FICTION / Family / Siblings. | JUVENILE FICTION / People & Places / Caribbean & Latin America. | JUVENILE FICTION / Nature & the Natural World / Environment.
Classification: LCC PZ7.5.E54 For 2017 | DDC [Fic]—dc23
LC record available at https://lccn.loc.gov/2016046561
ISBN 978-1-4814-9057-3 (hc)
ISBN 978-1-4814-9058-0 (pbk)
ISBN 978-1-4814-9059-7 (eBook)

With love for Curtis, who travels with
me, and with hope for all the young
wildlife conservation superheroes
of the future

Cada persona es un mundo.
"Each person is a world."

—Cuban folk saying

SUMMER 2015

A time of change

Family Disaster
~ EDVER ~

Miami, Florida, USA

I thought I was prepared
for any emergency. Fires, floods,
hurricanes, rogue gunmen, bombs,
and worse—we've covered them all,
in scary student emergency training drills.

We've shut down the school,
painted our faces with fake blood,
and practiced carrying one another
to an imaginary helicopter, moaning
and screaming with almost-real fear
as we pretended to survive crazy
catastrophes.

Nowhere in all that madness
did I ever imagine being sent away
by Mom, to meet my long-lost dad
in the remote forest where I was born
on an island no one in Miami
ever mentions without sighs,
smiles, curses, or tears . . .
but travel laws have suddenly changed,
the Cold War is over, and now it's a lot easier
for divided half-island, half-mainland

Cuban American families
to be reunited.

Mom is so weirdly thrilled,
it seems suspicious.
From the moment she announced
that she was sending me away to meet Dad,
I could tell how relieved she felt to be getting
a relaxing break from her wild child,
the troublemaker—me.

If she would listen, I would argue
that it's not my fault a racing bicycle
got in my way while I was playing a game
on my phone and skateboarding at the same time.
That's what games are for—entertainment, right?
Escape, so that all those minutes spent gliding
home from school aren't so shameful.
As long as I stare into a private screen,
no one who sees me
knows
I'm alone.

Tap, zap, swipe,
the phone makes me look as busy
as someone with plenty of friends,
a kid who's good at sports
instead of science.

In that way, I'm just like Mom, who hardly ever
looks up from her laptop on weekends.
She just keeps working like a maniac,
trying to rediscover lost species.

She's a cryptozoologist, a scientist who searches
for hidden creatures, both the legendary ones
like Bigfoot, and others that no one ever sees
anymore, simply because they're so rare
and shy, hiding while terrorized by hunters,
loggers, and poachers who sell their stuffed
or pinned parts to collectors.
Yuck.

But what if there's more?
What if Mom's real reason for peering
into her secret online world
is flirting to meet weird guys
who might not even be
the handsome heroes
shown in their photos . . . ?

What if she's dating,
and that's why she needs
to get rid of me, so she can go out
with creeps
while I'm away?

Our Fluttering Lives
~ LUZA ~

La Selva, Cuba

Green
all around me,
blue
up above,
and now my little brother
is finally on his way
to visit!

I've heard about Edver all my life,
from Abuelo, who misses his daughter—my mamá—
and from Papi, who speaks so mournfully of a time
when we all lived together as a family, rooted
in our forest, and winged
with shared dreams.

Now, as I step down to a clay bank where clouds
of blue butterflies have landed, brightness pulses
as the radiant insects sip dark minerals from mud,
performing a dance of hunger
called puddling.

Las mariposas—the butterflies—remind me
of miniature angels, skyborne, glowing,
magical and natural at the same time.

Do they know how fragile and brief
their airborne lives
will be?

After we travel to the city to meet my brother
at the airport, maybe I'll come back to this mossy
riverbank and sculpt a vision of people
with upside-down wings
beneath leafy green trees
rooted in sky. . . .

Or even better, I could just stand here and wait
for a tiny *colibrí* to arrive, a hummingbird no bigger
than a bee, the world's smallest bird, one of the many
living treasures that make Papi such a great
wildlife superhero, protecting our forest's
rare creatures
from the hunger
and greed
of poachers.

Saying Good-Bye to My Real Life

~ EDVER ~

On the last day of school before summer vacation,
I move like a shadow, trying to hide from all the kids
who saw that video of me crashing my skateboard
into the racing bike.

If I ever learn how to code my own truly cool game,
I'll fill it with shadow people whose feelings
can't be
seen.

Tomorrow I'll fly to Cuba.
Maybe getting away is a good thing.
If I stayed home, all I would do
is hide in my room
and play games
alone.

Raro

~ LUZA ~

¡Qué raro! How strange!

Yes, it feels truly surrealistic
to set out traveling like this,
happily ready to meet a stranger
and call him
my brother.

I hope he feels the same way about me.
Rare.
Like a forest bird
in the city.

The Isolation of Islands

~ EDVER ~

The plane lands.
A flight attendant leads me to a line.
Questions.
Answers.
Another fidgety wait.
More questions.
I show my passport.
My backpack is inspected.
The dissecting microscope
is passed around by men and women
in uniforms, some blue, others green,
until eventually everything
is returned to me
instead of stolen.

I sigh with relief,
but by now I'm so nervous that all I want to do
is calm my mind with the soothing clicks, zaps,
and whooshes of electronic dragon flames
in my favorite game, an online world
filled with griffin slobber,
troll breath, and the oozing farts
of lumbering ogres.

Imaginary animals are almost as bizarre
as the real ones, like that iridescent green

jewel cockroach wasp
I wrote about
for a nonfiction
book report.

The wasp injects poison into a roach's brain,
turning the bigger insect into a zombie
that can be ridden like a horse,
using the antennae as reins,
until they reach the wasp's nest,
where guess what, the obedient roach
is slowly, grossly
eaten by squirming
larvae.

No beeps or ringtones now.
No web of games and calming clicks.
No Internet at all, for researching
hideously fascinating natural stuff.

Being phoneless is my punishment
for that stupid bicyclist's injuries,
but Mom says I wouldn't be able to find
cell phone signals in Dad's forest anyway,
and hardly anyone on this entire island
has ever been on the Internet.

So I might as well be visiting the distant past
instead of a geographic curiosity, this antique place
where I was born.

All around me, Havana's José Martí Airport
bustles with joyful, abruptly reunited families,
all the shrieks,
sobs, and hugs
of long-lost relatives
as they find one another
for the first time in ten, twenty,
or fifty years.

I miss my phone.
How can such a loud island
be as electronically silent
as prehistory?

Futurology

Papi is so dedicated to patrolling our forest
that he won't leave for even one day.

That's why the villagers call him *el Lobo*—the Wolf.
He never gives up when he's tracking a poacher
who wants to eat a rare parrot, or steal
a bee-sized hummingbird
and sell it
as a pet.

So Abuelo and I are the only ones
who make the long trip to meet my brother
at the airport.

Fortunately, my grandpa knows how to find rides
the whole way, as we bump and rattle along potholed roads
in old cars already crowded with other hitchhikers,
all of us weary after an ordeal of waiting, sweating,
and praying
beneath the blazing sun.

This is *verano*, summer, the rainy season,
but for some unknown reason, we're in the middle
of our island's worst drought.
Is it climate change, the disaster Papi
keeps talking about?

11

Rivers of clouds
above rivers of water
have suddenly dried up,
leaving tropical parts
of the world
uncertain.

To pass the time, I imagine a future
of cave-dwelling, toolmaking rats
that will someday rule everything
unless deforestation
is stopped.

What a dilemma, Abuelo points out—we need
transportation, but we also want limitations.
We need farmland, but we can't chop down
all the wild, natural treasure of trees.

Drought in the rainy season is this year's curse.
Last year we had too many foreign tourists
stealing plants from our forest to use
as medicines, or to plant the prettiest orchids
in greenhouses, or simply because people
are greedy, and Papi can't patrol
every trail
all the time.

Even a wolf
needs a pack,
a team.

If only Mamá had never left.
Together, the two of them
could have been
fierce.

Bigfoot and Other Possibilities

If Mom weren't a cryptozoologist,
I probably wouldn't be a science nerd.
Maybe I would have more friends,
play on a team, get invited to parties,
and hang out at skate parks,
instead of crashing into bicyclists.

Mom travels the world looking for animals
that might not exist, and others that were firmly
believed to be extinct, until they were suddenly
rediscovered, becoming Lazarus species,
like that dead guy in the Bible
who was brought back to life—a miracle,
only these rare creatures have been found
by the hard work of stubborn scientists
who keep on and on, searching.

The Vu Quang ox, for instance.
It's a unicorn look-alike
in Vietnam and Laos.

It was classified as gone, then rediscovered,
and now it's endangered again, because the forest
where it lives
is shrinking.

So I guess if Mom ever finds Bigfoot or the yeti
or the Loch Ness monster, she'll have to list them
as threatened.

She says there are only two possible
twenty-first-century attitudes
toward nature:
1. Use it before you lose it.
2. Protect it while you can.

In an effort to make me love the father
I don't remember, she tells me he's a superhero,
the perfect example of a wildlife protector,
sacrificing everything to guard a single
mountaintop, along with all the bugs,
birds, bats, snakes, and lizards
that live there.

When she talks about him, her voice
slowly grows a little bit amazed, as if he's
a hidden fossil washed to the surface
by flash floods.

I wish she would talk about me that way
instead of urging me to go play outdoors
like a kid half my age.

She says it doesn't make sense,
the way I love science but don't know
how to explore.

Mom doesn't make sense either,
like right before the Miami airport
when she told me I'd soon meet
someone special—a surprise,
but she said it isn't Dad,
and she just got quiet
after I demanded
details.

I've never been a fan of Mom's
spontaneous surprises.
They're usually embarrassing,
upsetting, or worse,
like that time when she made me
change schools without warning,
or the Christmas when cousins
from far away tried to visit
and she refused to open the door,
insisting that she needed
to work.

What will it be this time?
I don't even want to make myself
dizzy and miserable
trying to guess.

Fragmentology
~ LUZA ~

When poor people hitchhike,
each ride is a gathering of attitudes.

Some whine about hunger.
Others share fruit.
Many sing; others remain silent
or tell wild stories, making up
fantastic lies.

Abuelo just speaks quietly, privately,
trying to prepare me for meeting my brother.
Why did the mother I can barely remember
choose Edver to go north with her,
while leaving me so far
behind?

Two fragments, two children, divided up
like leftovers
after a big picnic.
It happens all the time in Cuba,
families breaking up
into tiny remnants, like feathers
carried by wind
long after the bird
has died.

If I'm going to be a broken wing,
let me flutter at least once
before the magic
is lost.

Face-to-Face
~ EDVER ~

Beyond the airport's noisy baggage carousel,
a skinny old man holds up a sign with VERDE,
my real name, the word that didn't change
until kindergarten in Miami, when everyone
made fun of me for being called Green.

So I reversed it, only I couldn't pronounce
Edrev, so it turned into Edver.

Now, as if he knows the real me—a nerdy kid
named for the color of forest trees—Abuelo hugs me
fiercely, then grabs my backpack, chattering
rapidly, Cuban-style, as he leads me out to a blaze
of melting asphalt, where colorfully painted
antique cars are lined up all over the parking lot
in gleaming rows, like life-sized toys
for grown-ups.

Tu hermana, Abuelo says,
shoving me into the arms of a girl
so close to my age
that we could be twins.

¿Hermana?
Sister?

As far as I know,
I've always been
an only child!

Trying to pretend that I know
what's going on, I sort of hug her,
then bob my head like a bouncing ball,
barely listening
to her questions.

All I can do is think—really, Mom?
So this was your big surprise?

So many lectures about how to behave
on this island, but my mother never even bothered
to mention that I have *una hermana*, a sister,
my sibling, a mystery, puzzle, riddle. . . .

¿Por qué? Why? Don't I deserve simple truth
instead of complicated, *loca*-crazy
genius-Mom
selfishness?

There's only one way to survive
this sudden sister shock—pretend
I don't
care.

Rediscovered

I can't believe she never told him.
I've known about Edver all my life!

The ride to our *tía*'s house
in a rattling old taxi
now feels like a journey
across warped time
and empty space,
light-years of confusion
condensed into just a few
harsh minutes.

This whole city of La Habana is crumbling,
fronts of houses painted bright colors
while the backs are like skeletons, open
to a blaze of sky wherever parts of walls
are missing.

When we pass along the edge of the rough gray
coral stone Malecón seawall, I stare at teenagers
who dance around in groups, or sit alone,
sadly watching endless waves
as the blue water rolls toward Miami.

I imagine they're dreaming of travel,
just like Mamá, when she left home
without me.

My brother
absorbs our shared
sibling shock
by staying busy
instead of talking to me.

Eyes anxious, fingers nervous, he empties
his backpack, exposing gifts of such value
that I can hardly believe the dazzling show.

Soap, shampoo, lotion, all the things
that are so impossible to find here in Cuba.

Like a magician revealing a rabbit,
Edver unpacks a microscope—exactly the kind
Papi has always wished for, a dissecting scope
that will magnify delicate antennae, mandibles,
and wings, exposing all the secrets of insects.

Then, Edver begins to wave his hands around
like whirlwinds as he describes—in a language
neither wholly Spanish nor completely *inglés*—
the best way
to slap
a blob of dust
onto a thin glass slide, then slip it under
the amazing microscope's magical lens
so that we can detect a whole spider
the size

of a mosquito's
eye.

¡Increíble!
Incredible!
And yet, I believe him, just as I believe
in this impossibly marvelous reality of powerful
binoculars that my brother hands to me, declaring
that they're a special gift just for me, from our mother . . .
even though from his eyes I can tell
she said nothing about me.
Nothing at all. *Nada.*

Sister Shock
~ EDVER ~

At our friendly aunt's crumbling house,
I demonstrate biological detective work
using the dissecting scope
as I try to think of easy ways
to play games of amazement
with this mysterious puzzle
of a long-lost
instantly rediscovered
Lazarus sister.

I soon learn that dust mites don't impress Luza,
so I yank a dark strand from my head,
and sit down to show clear differences.
My hair is curly, hers straight.
Maybe we're not related after all, but we do
have the same reddish-brown skin, black eyes,
fierce glares, and reversed names.
Luza
started as Azul.
Blue.

Leave it to Mom to introduce us
by letting us figure out our own version
of truth.
Adopted?
Half?
Foster?

We seem so close in age,
but Abuelo and his sister—
our *tía*, a great-aunt—
both insist that Luza and I
are only one tiny
barely noticeable
year
apart.

That makes her twelve,
practically a teenage
stranger.

I'll definitely need this microscope
to find any bizarre little ways
that we might turn out to be
similar enough to ever hope
for some sort
of unusual
family disaster
friendship.

Or do I even want to understand Luza
and why Mom left her?
Wouldn't it be easier
to just pretend that this girl
is a stray quirk of nature,

like one of those half-unicorn
half-human centaurs
in my dragon game?

Microscopic
∼ LUZA ∼

I don't care about peering at a sliver
of dark curl from Edver's messy
bird's-nest head.

He's only eleven.
The difference between his age
and mine
is like the gap between believing
in rabbits
that spring from magicians' hats,
and knowing
that I can create my own
form of power, *lo real maravilloso*,
marvelous reality—a style my teacher calls
magic realism.
Art.
Sculpture.
Architecture.
Dreams made visible!
Shapes molded from mud, trash, junk,
all sorts of wasteful ugliness turning beautiful
simply from contact with creative human hands,
my fingers and palms hungry for meaning,
especially when this ordinary world
makes no sense.

So while Tía coats her face with a gift of lotion,
and Abuelo peers into the treasured microscope,
I gaze out a window with these new binoculars,
feeling even more alone than before I met
my wealthy *hermano americano*
with his fancy presents
and luxurious sports shoes.

Those basketball shoes he wears
probably cost as much as Abuelo's
entire annual retirement pension—six dollars
each month, and six times twelve months makes
seventy-two *dólares* per year, or as we *cubanos*
like to joke, *setenta y dos dolores*, painful sorrows,
not *dólares*, not money. Just a trick of spelling,
but it makes a huge difference.

This view from my aunt's window is almost
as tragic as my disappointing brother.

Tumbled balconies.
Crumbled sidewalks.
On both edges of the jaggedly potholed street,
banana and avocado trees send powerful roots
down into broken concrete, where tiny rootlets
grip slim cracks and split the hardness,
forcing this city world to make room
for natural growth.

On a peeling garden wall, someone has painted
a mural of upside-down-flowerpot hats
worn by people who don't seem aware
that jungle vines spill out over the brims,
with coiled tendrils clinging to eyes and ears,
making everything green, as if nature
is reclaiming lost territory.

The art festival must have started!
Someday soon, maybe my trash statues
will be included, all my tiny traces of hope
emerging from mosaics of broken things,
ugly things, microscopic shards
of possibility.

Rules
~ EDVER ~

Don't talk politics.
No showing off.
Never eat too much.
No gross jokes.
Never brag about owning
a lot of modern stuff
or being able to afford
to fix broken parts
of our house,
or the way
we shop
for unlimited mounds of groceries
in magnificent, overflowing
supermarkets.

Those were just a few of Mom's stern orders
when she dropped me off
at Miami International Airport
and let me figure out everything else on my own—
airport security, departure gate, and then
the arrival: passport, customs, questions.

So I'm trying to be mature and obey
every rule, just to show that I'm truly
responsible, so that maybe she'll
give me my phone back.

Avoiding politics is easy, because I never really
understood why the small country of my birth
and the huge nation of my daily life
ever hated each other so much
anyway.

Most of the other instructions are even easier.
I can't be a show-off without my phone,
since my only real skill is flying around
in dragon form, torching snotty trolls
with blazing flames that send my score
soaring.

Burps, farts, ogre poop,
even the funny parts of that game
aren't available over here.

All I have is my own sense of humor,
jokes that I have to keep secret, as I imagine
my sister in armor,
a clumsy knight who can't ride
her racing snail, a swift creature that hops
on one thick, slimy leg. . . .

Pretending I'm not hungry is something else,
a painful challenge, almost torture.

Mom warned me that while Tía is an eye surgeon,
doctors in Cuba only get twenty dollars
per month, just like everyone else.

So I'm not supposed to fill my belly
with her precious food rations—the carefully
measured amounts of rice, beans, and bread
that every islander receives.

I'd gobble at least three burgers
if I were home, and I'd be playing on my phone
while Mom stares at her laptop, but instead,
I'm stuck here at this unnaturally noisy table,
surrounded by people who talk, talk, talk,
instead of
politely
ignoring
one another.

My Spanish is fine, but I don't know all the gestures
and facial expressions.
Each time my sister rolls her eyes, it looks
like a secret message
written in code,
because she has at least fifty different
eyebrow positions for showing how disgusting
she thinks my game is
after listening to my enthusiastic Spanglish
description.

Qué bárbaro, Abuelo says, laughing
as I chat about green elf *dientes*
and the stinky *dedo del pie* fungus
of giant centipedes.

Bárbaro means cool, not barbaric,
so I know my grandpa has a sense
of humor, at least when it comes
to elf teeth and toe fungus.

After that, Abuelo and I keep dreaming up
truly cool gross stuff, and then we switch
to amazing scientific facts, like *el almiquí*,
a species of solenodon found nowhere else
on Earth, only in the wild parts of Cuba.

Everyone thought the strange little nocturnal
underground animal was extinct, until my grandpa
was part of a team of biologists who rediscovered
exactly
one
survivor.

They named the lone *almiquí* Alejandrito,
because one animal is an individual, not just a group.

Alejandrito had poisonous saliva, so Abuelo
couldn't touch his rat-shaped body or pointy
cartoon nose, for fear of getting bitten.

So he just watched the little creature
from a distance,
taking photos and scribbling notes,
back in the slow days
before computers and cell phones,
using film and a pen.

The good news is that just three years ago, in 2012,
seven more Cuban solenodons were discovered!
So it looks like this is one more Lazarus species
that actually stands a chance of real-life
survival.

When Luza suddenly wanders
into the conversation, she comments
on how shadowy the negatives of Abuelo's old photos
look, like a ghost animal captured on paper,
an eerie memory of the last male *almiquí*
searching for a lonely
female,
only it wasn't the last after all
so no one should ever lose
hope.

It's rule number one of cryptozoology.
Never be certain of total extinction.
Always remain willing to accept
amazement.

Maybe that's how I'll try to think of Luza,
as someone who claims to be my relative,
but is really just a living fossil, left over
from my parents' dead marriage.

Resolver

Resolve.
Solve problems.
Invent.

It's the way Papi taught me to adapt
to scarcity and hardships.

No soap?
Trade part of your rice rations
with a neighbor who receives gifts from Miami.

Not enough food?
Grow bananas and avocados on the sidewalk.

Vanishing wilderness?
Appoint yourself guardian of a forest, patrol
on your horse, carve a rifle from wood,
frighten poachers into thinking
you have bullets.

Disappointing long-lost brother
whom you almost wish you'd never
rediscovered?

Ignore him, and imagine
a more satisfying crypto-sibling

hidden deep inside your own
private mind,
sculpted and painted
from daydreams,
like the secret wishes
of some other
more generous
world
in a more serene
time.

Life in the Electronic Stone Age
~ EDVER ~

Noticing that my aunt has a computer
but no Internet
is like being on a planet
in the same enormous universe
as Earth,
but so many light-years away
that I'll never
be able to return
home.

There are old movies, jazzy music,
and exactly two games, silly ones
for little kids, not even worth playing.

So instead of staying cooped up
in that boring house, I agree to walk around
with Luza, looking at all the old junk art she calls
magic realism.

Statues at the Art Festival
~ LUZA ~

Red tongues pierced by swords,
rooster-people, centaurs, mermaids,
children shaped like boomerangs.

That last sculpture is easy to interpret.
The boomerangs are Miami kids like Edver,
taken away by grown-ups and now sent back
to meet their abandoned families
for the first time.

Why didn't our mother invite me to Florida
instead of sending my brother here
on his own, a confused boomerang boy
traveling
alone?

Lost but Not Found Yet

~ EDVER ~

Statues of centaurs and mermaids
make me think of Mom, with her grants
for studies of obscure species
that were believed to be gone forever
until a few survivors were found
by various international
research teams.

Terror skinks in New Caledonia.
Painted frogs in Colombia.
The Lord Howe Island stick insect, known only
from one shrub on Ball's Pyramid islet,
the world's most isolated lump of coral.
A giant Palouse earthworm,
three feet long, pale, and squirming,
assumed to have been killed off
simply because it buried itself
fifteen feet deep, where no one ever
thought to search.

Mom isn't picky about which creatures
she photographs and describes
for scientific and popular magazines,
just as long as they're Lazarus species,
proving that natural miracles are possible.

Borneo, Ecuador, Brazil—why doesn't she ever
take me with her on adventurous work trips?

If I'm old enough to travel to Cuba alone,
then I'm wise enough to be trusted
in other jungles.
Right?

She can't hold the whole bicycle-skateboard-phone
crash
against me
forever.
Can she?
Maybe meeting Luza and Dad is some sort of test!
If it is, I'll pass; just watch. I'll be careful.
Or maybe Mom has a boyfriend, or she's a spy,
or she's cryptic herself, hiding because of
some terrible
secret.

The Warmth of Coldness
~ LUZA ~

I stroll into an unusual statue
that's actually just a huge blue glass cube
with a person-sized opening on one side.

From inside all that blueness, the whole city
looks like refreshing sky, but this trapped air feels
so hot and stuffy that I rush right back out
to explore the next exhibit, an artificial beach
built just across from the real one.

Best of all, on a corner near the seawall,
some rich foreign artist has constructed
an ice rink!

Hot and cool, *caliente y fresco*,
a temperature duel . . .

My soul turns toward poetry, the only way
to build a breezy sky-sculpture
inside my heated mind.

Spin!

~ EDVER ~

Abuelo says the rink is a symbol of the recent
thaw in Cold War hostility between Cuba
and the US, but my sister calls it marvelous reality,
and I just think it's icy weirdness, like everything else
in my life.

Still, the temptation is too great to resist, so we wait
in a long line of strangers who take turns
borrowing skates—some look like European tourists,
but most are locals who've never seen ice unless
it was in a freezer, or a snow cone.

Twirling makes me dizzy enough to fall
but I don't, because a smiling fisherman
lets me and Luza both hang on to a pole
that helps us balance, while he pulls us to
the edge of the rink, sliding
toward safety.

Divided
~ LUZA ~

One fisherman's friendliness
saved us from crashing . . .
but right across a wide avenue,
standing on the seawall,
skinny men send colorful kites
out over the waves, delivering hooks
into the gaping mouths of distant fish.

In this land of *inventar y resolver*,
even a child's toy can be transformed
into a tool, by someone who is
hungry.

Two worlds.
One for tourists.
The other for everyone else.

Abuelo helps me show my cold brother
the tangled combination, with quaint
old streets where costumed dancers
called *los Gigantes*—the Giants,
leap and swirl on stilts,
while raggedy women
beg for soap,
and starving dogs
follow bored children

as they wait for their parents,
who stand in endless ration lines
just so they can collect
one fist-sized roll of bread
per person
per day.

While we're away from home,
Abuelo and I can't get our rations,
and we don't have much money,
but we wouldn't feel right
being fed by Tía for more
than one day, so I announce
that I'm hungry, just to see
what my rich foreign brother
will do.

Confusion
~ EDVER ~

I don't understand girls.
My sister wants me to buy food,
but as soon as she sees how much money
Mom gave me, she roars into anger-mode
just as abruptly as if someone had flipped
a switch.

All of this would have been easier if our mother
had bought a special gift for Luza on her own,
instead of just giving me those binoculars
for myself, then putting me in a position
where it seemed natural to pretend
that they were a present for Luza.

I'm getting pretty tired of trying to meet
expectations.

If I had my phone, it would be so easy
to turn into a dragon
and escape.

Wealth

~ LUZA ~

When half of a family is rich
and the other half is poor,
how can the two parts ever feel
united?

My brother claims that in Miami
he's barely average, with nothing
but a cell phone and skateboard,
surfboard, games, clothes, food,
a computer, and plenty
of television.

That's all he's ever owned, he explains,
with a deep sigh that makes him sound
helpless.

I guess I can figure out the rest.
No Papi, no Abuelo, no forest.
It's hard to believe, but he swears
that he envies me!

Survivors

~ EDVER ~

I survived emigration—the leaving of a country,
and immigration—the entering of another place,
but Luza survived
staying.

We're the same, in that one way,
our decisions made for us by grown-ups
long ago.

To keep myself from crying in front of
my tough big sister, I think of the sixty million bison
killed in the US in the 1870s, and how just one
man, a Kalispel Indian named Walking Coyote,
made such a difference by rounding up
thirteen survivors
to start his own herd.

He was a wildlife conservation superhero
long before saving animals from extinction
became popular, and now there are plenty
of bison again, but only because one person
was smart enough to plan ahead.

It's the same with California condors,
extinct in the wild by 1987, then brought back
by superhero zookeepers, who bred and babied

the last twenty-seven captives, even training them
to stay away from trash so they didn't
swallow poison.

Sometimes I watch condor chicks
in their wild nests, spied on by a webcam
that makes everyone feel like a scientist.
Is that the sort of thing Mom does
when she travels, sets up those cameras
then sits back and watches?

Why can't she pay as much attention to me
as she does to birds and bugs? Like those last
two huge Lord Howe Island stick insects that had her
so fascinated, when they were zoo-bred,
and soon exploded
into a population
of eleven thousand eggs
that yielded seven hundred
survivors.

Now the insects will need to be protected
from rats, if they're ever released back
into the wild, on the world's smallest island,
where they were found under a single shrub
at the top of the only rocky peak.

Those rats came from ships,
and ate the insects because they were
big, and as crunchy as lobsters.

That's how I feel sometimes,
huge and strong because I'm eleven,
but also weak and vulnerable
because I'm
me.

Weirdness
~ LUZA ~

Whenever we switch to English, my brother
uses words like *strange*, *bizarre*, *creepy*, *eerie*.

I want to think that it's just beautiful magic realism,
the way
our mother
took one of us
and left
the other.

But I can't.
I know it's not marvelous reality,
but cruelty, or selfishness, or illogical
weirdness, some variation on the theme
of survival
for herself.

Just imagine!
Edver says she leaves him with babysitters
from an agency, sometimes for weeks, or even
one whole month at a time, strangers,
different immigrant women
from Haiti, Romania, or Korea,
people Edver has to pretend
to understand.

So maybe I was the lucky one all along,
even though when I think about
growing up with a mother,
I still can't help wondering
how her voice would have
sounded, singing
a lullaby.

Blackout
~ EDVER ~

My first Cuban *apagón*.
I've heard of them forever.
Lights out.
No electricity at all.

Dark streets.
Voices, instead of faces.
The sounds of people walking
beside an eerie clip-clop
of horse-drawn vehicles
at midnight.

Only a few occasional headlights.
Old cars grumbling, as if they expected
better roads, with signs and lights
instead of banana trees
and avocados.

Luza sets a rocking chair out on the sidewalk
under a canopy of rustling leaves, using
her new binoculars to stare up at a blaze
of glittering stars.
Fire in the sky, bundled up
like mysteries made of energy.

Watching the stars, she starts telling stories,
making them up as she goes along,

first talking about giant fireflies
and glow-in-the-dark dogs,
then turning each weird creature
into a poem or a song.

So this is what it's like, I realize—being young
and ancient at the same time, feeling prehistoric,
truly caveman cool in one way, but also
sweaty and tired and scared
right here in my real life.

Time travel.
Space travel.
Family travel.
They all seem equally odd—just that short flight
across the few dozen miles of ocean that separate
my world from my sister's.

Singing, Singing, Singing
~ LUZA ~

My voice isn't special,
but melodies and rhythms help me
fade from harsh reality
into a serenade
of dreams. . . .

Wondering, Wondering, Wondering
~ EDVER ~

Each song leads me into a fantasy
of family disaster.

Is the bicyclist I hurt really okay?
Because no else's thoughts and feelings
ever seemed this real until tonight,
when suddenly
I have nothing to hear
but voices.

Mind travel.
If only I could figure out how to visit Mom
and ask her why she's such a coward,
smart and bold in every way except facing up
to her abandonment of Luza. And now she's
sent me away, but she stayed right there
in Miami, defending me from lawyers
and lawsuits, while avoiding the only
family truth that really matters
to me and my
surprise sister.

On Our Way
~ LUZA ~

In the morning, we drink strong coffee,
hug Tía, and set off without tickets,
because all the buses and trains
are so crowded that we'd have to wait
a whole week.

So we hitchhike as usual,
on a roadside packed with people
whose faces are exhausted, their bags,
boxes, baskets, and bundles all piled up
in neat rows of patience.

Are there really places where every family
owns a car, and gasoline is plentiful,
and no one ever has to stand in line
to wait, wait, wait,
while sweating?

I imagine that if I lived in a land like that,
my art would be photographs of real life
viewed under the microscope,
or through the magic
of binoculars and telescopes,
instead of mosaics
pieced together
from trash piles.

Time Traveler

I can't believe we're hitching rides
like hippies in some old movie!

A boxy Russian Lada,
then a sleek 1957 Chevrolet,
horse-drawn Volkswagens,
flatbed farm trucks,
so many vehicles
take turns
carrying us,
moving us,
bringing me
closer
and closer
to meeting Dad. . . .

But what if he doesn't care?
He didn't even come to the airport.
Maybe he was glad that Mom took me away
when I was a baby—what if they didn't even
fight about the separation?

Dad probably chose Luza
because he knew I'd be trouble,
the kind of kid who crashes into strangers
while skateboarding.

Thinking all this yucky stuff
while riding in an oxcart
makes me feel like a zombie fossil,
one of those weird scientific curiosities
that gets eroded out of its own
layer of stone, then washes up
somewhere else, so that paleontologists
find dinosaur bones jumbled together
with woolly mammoths and cavemen,
creating the illusion of closeness in time,
but really they're just out of place,
tricky and mixed up.

Zombie fossils don't belong where you find them.
Just like me.

I'd call home and demand a quick return flight
to my real world, if only I had a phone
and a signal.

Strangers
~ LUZA ~

I'm not afraid of the drivers who pick us up.
Some are foreign tourists in rented cars,
others just ordinary Cubans
who need help paying for gas.

Many of the sugarcane fields we pass
are overrun by thorny scrub, because tractor fuel
is so scarce that working the soil is impractical
unless you have mules or oxen.

But everything isn't ugly and hopeless. . . .
When we pass towering mango trees,
I spot a migration of magnificent
yellow-and-black-striped
tiger swallowtail butterflies
that swirl through the air
like daydreams!

Maybe science isn't so boring after all.
If my sculptures never get exhibited, I could be
an entomologist like Papi, studying caterpillars
with their amazing ability
to grow and change.

I wonder if butterflies recognize themselves
while they're still all wrapped up

inside motionless cocoons,
waiting,
waiting,
waiting,
like hitchhikers
on a lonely roadside.

Coevolution

~ EDVER ~

Mom taught me that whenever a narrow flower
evolves a longer and longer shape,
the beaks of hummingbirds
gradually change too.

All it takes
is a few million years.
So now, as we bump along in a horse-drawn wagon,
I picture invisible satellite signals beaming down
from outer space, useless in this isolated place
where people still depend on one another's
voices
for entertainment.

Could I ever adapt to these electronic limits?
I guess all it would take is the rest of my life
to learn how to survive in phoneless
silence
like my sister.

Quiet Hills
~ LUZA ~

Nightfall,
the clip-clop
of horse hooves.

Rhythmic flashes
from dancing
fireflies.

Around each curve
the rising moon.

Abuelo's long folktales, his stories
of glow-in-the-dark dogs and magical horses. . . .

My brother's fingers twitch as if he's longing
to send phone messages back to his real home.

What was Mamá thinking, forcing *un americano*
to spend time with *los cubanos*, sharing
our quiet isolation?

Ghostly

~ EDVER ~

The missing phone feels
like a phantom limb
after an amputation
during a disaster.

No painkillers.
No antibiotics.
Just wishes.

Time
is so much slower
here.

So I lean into the night breeze
inhaling minutes, hours,
light-years. . . .

Caged
~ LUZA ~

By morning, all three of us are talking about
convergent evolution.

Octopus eyes and human ones,
separately developed, yet eventually
becoming similar.

Is that how Edver and I ended up
so much alike
yet also completely different?

When we finally reach a town at the foot
of our mountains, all the morning markets
are already bustling with hungry women
trying to sell handmade lace to tourists,
musicians playing songs in exchange
for soap, vendors chanting about ice cream,
and a poacher offering a rare parrot,
trapped inside
a tiny cage.

Sharing

The eyes of the parrot
haunt me.

I pull cash out of my pocket
and buy the bright green bird,
planning to set it free as soon as we reach
the edge of town, but when I flash
all that American money,
I know
I've forgotten my instructions.
Never
show off!

So I spend a bunch more on good food
and strong coffee, half of it bought
in a fancy restaurant for tourists,
and the rest from a street vendor
who sells slices of pineapple
and fresh guava pastries.

I buy so much that there's plenty to share
with all the other hitchhikers
on our final ride in the back of a beat-up
old Russian army truck, four-wheel drive,
roaring, rumbling, and forceful,

like a dangerous beast
in a scary story.

From my lap,
the caged parrot
stares at the sky, then at me,
as if he's wondering
how he ever ended up
in the same sad world
as selfish
humans.

Climbing

~ LUZA ~

We roll and sway all the way
            up the mountain,
winding through dust,
            our forest so dry
                  on this fever-hot day
during a season when rain
                              normally pours.

Drought.
Climate change.
Sorrow.
No, I can't stand those sorts of thoughts,
not constantly—so for now, I concentrate
on the beauty all around me, tree-sized ferns
with their feathery greenness, coffee farms,
shady jungle, and somehow, the survival
of waterfalls.

Even in the village where I go to school,
everything looks so dazzling
today.

Rare

I've never had a pet.
Mom travels too much.

So when I decide to open the door
of the cage, I feel a twinge of envy.

My sister has probably owned
every kind of animal that most kids
get to keep—dogs, cats, birds, fish. . . .

This parrot is brilliant, colorful—
white forehead, ruby cheeks, emerald body,
royal-blue wings, intelligent eyes.

Abuelo says it's a Cuban amazon,
an endemic species, meaning that it isn't found
anywhere else on Earth, just here, right here,
this island, this jungle, the one place Luza
calls "our forest," like some sort
of family inheritance,
a treasure.

Home!

~ LUZA ~

After the captive parrot rises up to join
its wild relatives, all the other hitchhikers
get off at various coffee farms, but we
keep going, the truck driver happy
to accept my brother's
foreign money
as payment
for reaching
the highest home
on our mountain.

We don't have to hike at all.
He drops us off right in front of the peeling
blue door.

Papi's horse and my pony are both here,
so that means no one is patrolling today.

I hope a poacher doesn't take advantage
and trap the freed parrot
all over again.

Home?

The house is cabin-sized,
with lemony yellow walls,
a red tile roof, and a faded blue door
that's ready for a paint job.

There are flowering trees everywhere,
red, pink, gold, white, and purple.
Was I really born here?

A horse, a pony, chickens, a wiener dog,
and strange, ratlike animals that I recognize
from Mom's photos—*jutías*, a relative of pikas
and marmots, but endemic to Cuba, just like
the parrot.
Unique.
Found nowhere else
on Earth.
As if this forest is its own
hidden world.
Cryptic.

Greeting

~ LUZA ~

Jutía, our skinny dog, rushes to greet Abuelo.
Dad's old white horse, Rocinante, whinnies.
My silvery pony, Platero, just keeps grazing.
He's lazy, just like the wild *jutías*
that stretch out on branches, half asleep,
enjoying the sunlight that reaches them
between pools of shade cast by red flame trees
and cacao shrubs, with those big pods
that contain the bitter beans
I'll soon be able to sweeten
for making chocolate.

Our vegetable garden is filled
with tonight's dinner, colorful bursts
of tomatoes, cucumbers, and melons,
all waiting for me to pick them
and make a cool
juicy salad.

When Papi steps out of the house,
I rush to hug him, but he soon lets go
and wraps his arms
around Edver.

Indoors, I greet the little tree frog
that always chirps from our bathtub,

and the lime-green-and-turquoise lizard
who perches on a wall above my bed,
pulsing his magenta throat patch.

If the frog and lizard remember me,
they don't show any more joy than Jutía,
a one-man dog
who only loves
Abuelo.

Meeting Dad
~ EDVER ~

He's tall, with curly black hair like mine.
I expected someone older, but he seems
energetic enough to be my big brother.

How should I talk to him?
English, Spanish, Spanglish,
or just truly cool scientific words,
all those Latin genus and species names
that Mom sprinkles into practically every
sentence?

He tries to hug me,
but I yank the microscope
out of my backpack
and fill his hands with its
hardness, so that he can't
pretend to love me
after all these years
apart.

Fumes

~ LUZA ~

My rude brother calls Mamá
from the old wall phone,
our home's only gadget
for communication.

It's the only phone I've ever known,
the one that I've never used for trying
to contact my mother,
even though she once wrote
me a letter, offering her number.

Why should she be included
in this awkward
little family reunion,
when she's the one
who chose
not to be here?

She must be asking to talk to me now,
because Edver tries to hand me the phone,
but no, no, no, I won't, even though she's all
I ever think of on my gloomiest days,
those mornings at school when I'm bored
and can't stop daydreaming
about how cruel she was
when she took

baby Edver
and rushed
away.

What good will it do to talk to her today,
bringing her voice close, while her heart
remains distant?

I feel like one of those dragons
in that strange video game
my brother always raves about,
with beasts that spew toxic smoke
long after the flames
of rage
vanish.

Abuelo has always described Mamá as a wildly
unpredictable person, the brilliant mind who moves
likes a storm in wind, with ideas of her own, ideas
that she treats like children, while treating
her real children
like passing thoughts
that can care for themselves
or merely fade away,
fruitless.

Now, Edver has added a new way to solve
the mystery of our unusual mother.
He says she's creatively crazed,

explaining that geniuses
often forget to notice
the people around them.

If only I could be
the daughter of a brainy
innovator
who also has
a heart.

The Next Morning
~ EDVER ~

Mosaics.
Masks.
Statues.
Painted boulders.
Pebble people with plastic
trash eyes.

My sad sister's sculpture trail—
the first place I explore on my own.
I've imagined this forest all my life.
Branches rising,
tangled up with sky.

My shoes leave zigzag prints
in fresh mud,
the softness of mist
from last night's damp clouds
almost as wet as real rain.

Mossy earth, snail shells,
the shimmering, dark eye-shine
of a bright orange oriole, and parrots,
so many green parrots wildly clacking
from the feathery fronds
of a towering
palm tree!

Maybe the bird
I set free
is up there right now,
calling down to thank me.

The Family Mosaic
~ LUZA ~

Going off on his own is an insult.

If he steps on my statues, I'll kick him.

These feelings are so disturbing.

Never before have I ever imagined such fury!

Temper and envy.
Envy and temper.

Like a chicken and her egg,
which comes first?

I can be just as rude as my foreign brother,
but what good would it do?

I'm just one broken shard of glass
in this sharp, glittering world
of separated
siblings.

Warnings
~ EDVER ~

Mom assured me that there are hardly any
big, scary animals in this jungle, just birds, bats,
iguanas, frogs, boa constrictors,
and those cute little *jutías*.
Pronounced *hoot-EE-ahs*
not *joot-EYE-as*
like Luza said
when she teased me
about knowing
more English
than Cubanness.

Mom warned me about the small size
of this forest's creatures because she thought
I'd be disappointed if I didn't get to see
monkeys, tapirs, and sloths,
all the tropical species you see
in rain forest books.

She's wrong!
I'm glad there aren't any poisonous vipers
or hungry jaguars, because I'm only brave
on a phone screen, not outdoors, where trying
to learn how to surf in Florida
made me so nervous about sharks
that I couldn't really enjoy

the roll of waves
or sparkle
of sunlight.

It's all I can do now to stay calm
while surrounded
by disease-carrying mosquitoes,
and ants—tons of ants, big ones in endless rows
marching as busily as an army, each one carrying
a sliver of leaf that looks like a green knife.

Instead of telling me there wouldn't be any
scary predators in this forest, Mom should've
warned me that I'd be stalked by my angry sister,
a glaring, staring, troll-eyed cave bear.

Usually I like being the dragon in a game,
but if I had my phone right now, I'd choose
a sword, and become an armored knight,
completely human, the most dangerous
animal
on Earth.

There's no weapon more frightening
than another person's
distrust.

No Warnings
~ LUZA ~

I didn't know what to expect,
because Papi and Abuelo haven't seen Edver
since he was a baby.

In the kitchen after breakfast, my brother
comes home as if he never left, then he shows off
his knowledge of microscope knobs and lenses,
while I wash dishes, and send my mind flying
back to a time when Abuelo
took me to visit a teenage cousin
who works on a crocodile farm
in coastal swamps.

Her job is painting splashes of yellow clay
onto the cheeks of tourists who come in boats
to see statues of the Taínos, *los indios* who thrived
in Cuba long ago, and who still are completely alive
in our own family's DNA.

I picture those spiral twists, the double helix
that geneticists found when they came to our forest
to study us—explaining that we're descendants
of survivors, our blood, saliva, and bones
all filled up with clues that show
how long we've been here.

Five, ten, maybe even thirty thousand years.
We're a Lazarus family, our ancestors classified
as extinct
by every history book
on Earth,
until DNA studies
proved that *los Taínos*
still exist.

So now my cousin's job is standing in a *caney*—
a palm-thatched longhouse—on a dry patch
of land surrounded by water, painting
the faces of foreigners who go there to see
marvelous statues left behind
by an artist.

Sculptures of people with names.
Individuals, not just a tribe.
Yaima, a little girl, Abey the crocodile hunter,
Cojimo, with his hairless dog, chasing furry *jutías*,
Tairona, hunter of ducks, and Guamo, the musician
who plays a conch shell,
Yarúa and Marien,
two children kicking a ball,
and Alaina the weaver girl,
her mother, Yuluri, spinner of wild cotton,
Colay, a man planting yuca,
Bajuala, the boy who talks to macaws,
Yabu, a farmer of corn, Guacoa, a man who lights fires,

Arima, a girl shaping clay, and Guajuma,
the woman who decorates ceramics.

Of all the statues, my favorite is Dayamí,
la muchacha soñadora, the girl who dreams.

Did Dayamí ever wonder about the future—
imagining her descendants, picturing me?

I always thought meeting my brother
would lead me toward Mamá, but now I see
that even if I had a way to reach Miami
I'd still be alone in certain ways, because now
when I daydream,
I no longer know
which way to face—
future or past,
Mamá's adopted
foreign shore
or my home,
this forest.

Truce

Abuelo and Dad make us sit down
and talk.

The discussion starts with confessions
of temper
and envy,
then moves on
to a confusing duel of visions
for our future—one home or two for me,
but no choices for my sister, because all she gets
is whatever she was born with, and no one
but our mother can ever afford to send Luza
on an overseas trip.

By the end of an hour, Abuelo is reciting poetry,
Luza answers with her own verses, Dad sings,
and I return to the reassuring microscope,
determined to figure out how many
diamondlike facets I can find
on a housefly's amazing
kaleidoscopelike
compound eye.

Maybe my sister's odd, complicated art works
aren't so bad after all.

I think I'm starting to understand her fascination
with magic realism.

Here in Cuba, everything seems all mixed up,
time going in circles, the past still alive
inside everyone's
mind. . . .

No wonder Mom cries while she writes
on her laptop, hiding her face by letting
her long hair swish like a curtain
at the end of a play
filled with smiling
happy actors.
Maybe she hates
being a lonely
genius.

Chores

~ LUZA ~

Gardening, cooking, grinding coffee,
grooming horses, gathering eggs,
waiting in food ration lines
down in the village. . . .

Edver admits that he has never done more
than clean his own room, make his bed,
and pretend to listen when teachers
tell him how to do his homework.

Somehow, he ends up with perfect grades,
while I study and study, never mastering
all the concepts of revolutionary history,
so that I only excel in art
and the underappreciated skill
of imagining.

Contests

No cell phone.
No ready-made games.
The evenings are just an endless stretch
of *telenovela* soap operas from Venezuela.

When we get tired of watching grown-ups
fall in and out of love, my sister and I begin
inventing new ways to defeat each other.

Luza is the best actor when it comes to imitating
an ogre, but I've been a dragon for so long
that I've perfected the illusion
of dangerous flames.

So we end up calling it a tie.
Equality.
A compromise.
Peace.

Play

I love telenovelas, but I also crave victory.
Sometimes our games are old-fashioned.
Edver wins at chess, but my hands swoop
like birds when we play dominoes with Abuelo.
My brother wins at cards, but I can kick a *fútbol*,
and when Edver invents a makeshift skateboard
from a slab of wood and some rickety
desk chair wheels, I balance so easily
that afterward, he admits he feels clumsy
trying to learn how to ride Papi's horse
and my pony.

But we're not ready to give up competing
and comparing, daring each other to leap
higher, jump farther, race faster,
and shout louder.

Are we friends yet?
Maybe.
Almost.

The Truth of Dare

The one thing we're really good at sharing
is adventure, so we sneak out at night to peer up
at owl eyes, and we scramble up slopes by day
to splash in rocky pools beneath waterfalls.

We take turns gathering bugs
to stare at under the microscope.
My prize is a hawk moth that looks
exactly like a hummingbird, and Luza's
is a cicada with eyes the color
of tomatoes.

But when we play truth or dare,
I'm not brave enough to reveal secrets,
so I claim all the imaginary prizes
for feats of foolishness, like jumping off
waterfall cliffs.

It's kind of funny how my courage starts
with cowardice.

Hovering
~ LUZA ~

Each time I dare my brother to call our mother
on the wall phone, I hover and listen, but she's
always gone,
traveling to some distant land,
her answering machine a long list
of destinations spoken in English.

"Hi, I'm doing fieldwork in Fiji, talk to you
when I get back.
Hey, I'm on a volcano in Japan, see you soon,
Edvercito.
Wow, this is my first trip to Argentina!
Hope you're having fun with *la familia*.
Hola. Tell your sister I'm sorry for everything,
and I promise we'll talk, oh, and remind Yoel
that I have big news for La Selva—all he needs to do
is fill out those forms, they should be there by now.
I sent them with a courier.
Give Abuelito a hug, and kiss Jutía,
if that funny old wiener dog is still alive.
By the way, after a great deal of back-and-forth
between lawyers, the bicyclist decided
not to sue after all, as long as I agree to pay
all the hospital bills, so listen, *m'ijo*, you got off easy
this time, but he could have pressed charges.
You would have been the least violent kid

in juvenile hall—in other words,
the most pummeled. (That means beat-up,
in case you haven't been studying
all those vocabulary words
I put in your backpack!)"

So much about Edver, but NOTHING about me.
Not one real message for my ears,
only that quick lie about being sorry,
and the feeble promise to talk.

If I could turn back time, I'd be two years old,
searching the forest again, trying to find
my mother, who had just abandoned me,
taking my baby brother. . . .

I'd locate her this time, then I'd reach up
and pummel her with my tiny
fists.

Forms?

What does Mom mean?
Dad won't explain.
He just grins and shrugs,
as if they share a secret.

Is this why she left him,
because he's so silent,
the quietest Cuban
who ever lived?

"Fill out the forms."
That could be anything!
Adoption, custody, foster parents,
or who knows what other form
of family torture?

Luckily, Dad feels so bad about leaving me
wondering
that he decides to spend lots of time with me
doing other things.

My favorite moments are the ones
filled with actions, instead of words.

We walk around the forest, studying bugs,
leaves, and seeds of all sorts, even peeking

inside holes in wood,
to find grubs and worms
that can be
identified.

El baile de los viejitos
~ LUZA ~

When Dad goes back to his solitary work,
and Edver once again feels left out, our shared
confusion
makes us grouchy.

We have to get away from our thoughts,
so Abuelo takes us down to the village,
all three of us mounted on big Rocinante,
while Dad goes off on his routine patrols
riding little Platero.

In town, we eat surprisingly well, considering
the general scarcity of food, because all we have to do
is stand around inside el Club de los Abuelos,
a senior center where white-haired ladies feed us
whatever they have—rationed rice, garden produce,
wild fruit, and sweets, all sorts of treats
made from homegrown sugar,
chocolate, spices, and coffee.

Next, we dance.
Abuelo is the one who invites me to star
in *el Baile de los Viejitos*, the Dance of Little Old Folks.

So I twirl and leap with a cane, pretending to sway,
lose my balance, almost fall, totter feebly,

move as if my back hurts, my bones creak,
my mind wavers, and still, despite all that pain,
I feel
so exhilarated
that the lively dance steps
ABSOLUTELY BURST
from my aching body,
while an ear-to-ear SMILE
never leaves my brightly painted
old lady lips!

Funny

~ EDVER ~

The secret of *el Baile de los Viejitos*
is making young dancers appear to be old,
not the other way around.

It's a really weird kind of humor,
the sort Abuelo loves, because instead of just
making fun of himself, he's also teasing us.

He says we'll be old someday, and then
we'll understand.

I don't really believe him, because the world
seems like such a mess that if this were a game,
I wouldn't expect to survive, but it's real life,
so I laugh out loud
each time my sister's cane
taps a loud rhythm
that matches the size of her clunky
thick-soled, old lady shoes!

Boys My Age

~ LUZA ~

I feel like a fantastic dancer
until other children show up,
but this awareness of the presence
of the grandsons of real old ladies
suddenly makes me self-conscious
about my white wig and flowered apron.

Introducing my brother to school friends
is a huge decision.

What if he offends them with his show-off
rich-kid shoes
and foreign ways?

But the girls are so excited to finally meet
un americano who isn't a tourist!

Everything has to be explained to Edver,
especially names, because islanders
had to give up saints' names
during the years when religion
was illegal, so now many parents
are still in the habit of inventing new words
instead of choosing old-fashioned ones
that carry all the risks of history.

Danía's name is a mixture of Daniel and María.
Yamily rhymes with the English word *family*,
because all her brothers floated away to Miami.
Dayesí—*da*, yes, *sí*—means yes, yes, yes
in Russian, English, and Spanish.
It's a name that grew out of the craziness
of never knowing whether poor little Cuba
would end up in the shadow of one enormous
bossy foreign nation
or the other.

I'm too shy to spend much time with boys,
but a dark-eyed dreamer called Yavi
loves to tease me,
so he follows me around,
pretending to be friendly,
when really all he wants to do
is show off his fancy clothes
and modern gadgets, all sent to him
by relatives in Florida.
His name means *Ya vi*, "I already saw,"
but he never says exactly what his mamá
looked at while she attached two old words
together, turning them into a new one.

As soon as Yavi meets my brother, I can tell
that they share the same sense of humor,
filling up any awkward silences
with fartlike noises and real burps.

Yavi's eyes make me nervous,
so I rush away from him, guiding Edver
on a tour of the ration shop, with its nearly
empty shelves, followed by a tourist store
overflowing with luxuries, and a restaurant
where foreigners come to drink
sweet mountain coffee, and eat
rare foods that the rest of us
can't afford, unless we grow
the vegetables ourselves,
and raise the chickens,
and gather
wild spices.

Connected!
~ EDVER ~

Staring girls with weird names
make me feel like racing away,
but Yavi says he owns a computer,
and has IntERnet—global, not just
the island's local IntRAnet!

So while my sister tries to show me things
she thinks are interesting—like her school,
a park, the post office, a church—all I can do
is hop up and down inside my mind
while I wait for a chance
to run across the street
with Yavi, and sit down
to face familiar flares
of dragon flames, roaring
from ravenous mouths. . . .

If there's a forbidden satellite dish,
it must be well hidden behind all those
flowering red flame trees, yellow hibiscus,
and purple jacaranda.

But the connection is dial-up,
soooooooo
SLOOOOOW
but still

so amazingly
satisfying!

Now here I am, right back where I belong,
inside my normal world, the cryptic one
that's hidden deep inside
this computer screen.

Nerviosa/Nervous
~ LUZA ~

I've never broken such an absolute rule.
Everyone knows *el* IntERnet is *peligroso*,
dangerous, forbidden, banned,
off-limits to the general public,
available only in certain places
to special people.

Rocking chairs, a lace tablecloth,
Yavi's dozing great-grandma, it all seems
so ordinary, except for the way my bold brother
taps his fingers on a magical keyboard
to make imaginary creatures appear. . . .

When he and Yavi finally finish
their endless game of growling battles,
I venture to ask the question that haunts me.
If I spell certain words, will I see Mamá's picture
and be able to write a letter that will reach her,
maybe even receive an answer, hear her voice
on paper, print it, and hold a mystery in my hand
forever?

Passwords

I know them all, because I'm the one
who used to help Mom set up her pages,
albums, profiles, and blogs, not to mention
spending plenty of lonely hours
spying on her, trying to see
who she knows,
chats with,
flirts with,
maybe even
dates.

Creeps?
Mean men?
Losers.

I wouldn't be surprised.
Why else would she keep her private life
so secretive lately, hiding some of it so well
that even I can't hack the new accounts,
break complicated codes, and find her friends'
unfamiliar faces?

When I see how many followers she has now,
I know she's been busy tapping away at her laptop
while sitting on beaches in Fiji, volcanoes in Japan,
and grassy savannahs in Argentina.

Grants, research, articles in science journals,
all of it is right here in front of me, a detailed record
of her movements and interests.

Nothing at all about the son she sent away
for a whole summer, or the daughter
she abandoned forever.

Luza is standing right behind me,
looking over my shoulder. I wonder
how she feels, seeing her absence
from Mom's online
mind.

Maybe the word *genius* needs
a new definition, something
that measures mountains of emotions,
not just separate, tiny
thoughts.

Scheming

Silent room.
Sorrowful reality.
What would Mamá say
if we unite
to invite her
to visit us?

Will she see our plea
as an opportunity
or a complaint?

I need a magnet to draw her close,
something to attract her scientific curiosity!

When I explain my idea to Edver, he shakes
his head slowly, then pauses, shrugs, grins,
and says that it's possible, maybe we could
really lure her, but only with a wildlife
emergency.

Name any animal, my wily brother suggests.
Nothing big, he adds.
We don't want her to see
that our newly discovered species
is a lie.

Jewel beetle?
Dragonfly?
Golden silk orb-weaver?
Tree frog?
Anole lizard?
Scorpion?

Gradually, a lost-and-found image drifts
back into my vision, a memory of tiger swallowtail
butterflies, soaring between mango trees
while we were hitchhiking,
such a colorful cloud
of striped wings. . . .

Edver stands up, tells me to sit down,
then shows me how to type NEW *PAPILIO*,
making everything capitalized, a SHOUT
for our mother's ATTENTION.

Papilio—the genus name of swallowtails!
I look over my shoulder and see Edver
smiling—he approves, so he must
actually think this trick might work.

Now let's add the location, he instructs.
La Selva. The Jungle. On *la isla*,
but he warns me
not to name Cuba,
because that makes

the puzzle
too easy.

We've created a challenge,
a dilemma, a problem.
Will she solve it?
Does she play games?

There are so many jungles in the world,
so many islands, how will she know
which place we mean?

We haven't used our names,
and she won't recognize Yavi's
online account.

But Edver seems so confident.
He swears he understands how her mind works.
She'll see NEW *PAPILIO* and feel driven, he promises.

Obsessed, she'll need to find out if this might be
a Lazarus species, one that was extinct
until NOW, this moment
of magically real
rediscovery.

No Way

It's perfect.
A secret.
Right here on this familiar World Wide Web
of words, where nothing is ever really
private.

Mom will know which island we mean, won't she?
If anyone else sees it, they'll be confused, won't they?

My sister and I wait.
Electronic silence.
No response.
Mom's not reading her phone,
all those messages, comments, posts,
boasts, and praise from her friends
and from strangers.

So she must be out in another jungle
someplace remote, with no connection.

There aren't too many countries
where the Internet is still restricted,
but there are plenty of places without
any way to make contact.
Too poor.
Too isolated.

Too small.
Just huts.

When the maddening screen silence continues,
I grow restless and start to roam all over her pages,
until I notice her status: IN A RELATIONSHIP!!!
All caps.
Three exclamation marks.
Yikes, this is serious.

So that's it—the explanation for my surprise trip
to Dad's house. Mom must have sent me away
just so she could be alone with some guy.
Who is he, and why doesn't she want me
to meet him?
Maybe he hates kids.
Yeah, it was probably his idea
to get rid of me for the whole summer
or even longer.

Creepy
~ LUZA ~

Mamá's boyfriend is hideous, his face distorted,
the grin too big, like a giant staring into a river
where water becomes a rippling,
racing mirror.

Somehow, I feel like I might have seen him before.
Maybe in an article, one of those scientific magazines
Papi sometimes receives as gifts from traveling
researchers?

Edver explains that strange photos are the result
of taking one's own picture too close up—*un* selfie *feo*,
an ugly self-portrait, smug, arrogant, *presumido*,
stuck-up.

The distorted man's bulging bug eyes
seem to be admiring the camera,
instead of his beautiful *novia*.

But she's gazing at him.
Why?

Nothing

~ EDVER ~

During the minute we waste staring
at Mom's boyfriend,
NEW *PAPILIO*
has already been shared
by scientists on three continents.
So I quickly click delete.
Gone.
Extinct.
No more fake species
of beautiful rare butterfly.
My sister's message hurtles back in time
to that moment a few minutes ago,
before our tricky words existed.
But not really, because they've already
been shared, and probably printed,
spreading across the world
like polluted air.

Forget it, I tell Luza,
this was a waste,
she's not coming, Mom doesn't care,
we're on our own,
there's no way to distract
a brilliant person from her own stupidity
once she gets her imagination filled up
with nonsense.

Mom and I must be the reason
people invented
the phrase
one-track mind.

Each of us can be narrow enough
to follow a railway, trail, or road
straight into a crash
without noticing
danger.

Everything
~ LUZA ~

As soon as the words I typed are gone,
my brother and I return to the way we felt
about each other right after meeting.
Neither enemies nor friends, just two lives
that can never be truly close, because of the sea
in between.

We're like insects, bats, and birds,
all just as thoroughly winged,
even though they evolved separately.

Edver could have given my trick a chance,
but he's selfish, so what else can I send
to tempt Mamá?

Photos of sculptures—but no, I don't have
a camera, and anyway, I can imagine
that my mother might be horrified if she saw
all my muddy self-portraits decorated with trash,
a throwaway girl, her creation,
not mine.

Blame

Luza storms outdoors to play *fútbol*
with her friends, the soccer ball hurtling
away from her forehead
like a bullet.

No te preocupes,
Yavi's great-grandma says,
creaking up out of her rocking chair
to follow me outdoors,
where she drapes
a strand of beads
around my neck.

The beads are seeds.
She names them:
Fortuna. Luck.
Flor de amor. Flower of love.
Mal de ojo. Evil eye.

I thank her and touch each bead,
noticing that luck is big and glossy,
while the flower of love is small and light
with bracts that open like petals,
but evil eye is dark and shiny,
a night creature
creeping.

I don't want to keep
this eerie necklace,
but if I throw seeds away,
won't they sprout and grow
into blessings
or curses,
rooted?

Separate

~ LUZA ~

I let my brother find his own way home
while I play *fútbol* until I'm exhausted,
all the rage burned away and charred
into ashes of sadness.

Walking home alone feels right,
until the chuckle of a tocororo bird
helps me laugh at myself, his array
of red, white, blue, and green feathers
so cheerful that it's easy to forget
how impossible
it is for his species
to survive in captivity.

If you try to cage *un tocororo*
all you'll end up with is a memory
of lost wings.

Later

Stuck in the same house as my angry sister,
I avoid her by helping Abuelo identify bugs,
beetles, glittering as brightly as jewels.

Some are striped purple and green, others
pale yellow and deep red, but my favorite
is a species that is almost always silver,
until an occasional gold one is found.

Maybe gold is a mutation,
or just an oddity
created by climate change.

Imagine what a terrific
evolutionary advantage
that one gold beetle would have,
camouflaged in a thicket
of yellow flowering shrubs,
protected from predators
by pretending to be
invisible.

Mom always talks about biodiversity,
but I hardly ever listen carefully enough
to think about what she really means.

Now, my mind scrambles all over
the possibilities, picturing variety,
flora and fauna, humans, too,
so many variations,
a world of amazement
that shrinks each time a forest
vanishes, each tree such a wealth
of species that live on branches,
inside wood, down in leaf litter,
scurrying through shade,
gobbling fruit, swallowing seeds,
growing. . . .

Abuelo's room starts to feel like a museum.
There are stuffed birds here too, not just
pinned beetles.

There's an ivory-billed woodpecker
that has only been extinct in Cuba
for thirty years.

Mom was one of the last people to see it alive,
pecking at the bark of a palm tree above her head,
when she was little.

This bird might turn out to be a Lazarus species!
Someone—maybe me—could rediscover it,
and become famous as a wildlife conservation
superhero!

But there's a brilliant Cuban macaw, too,
extinct since the 1850s, and Abuelo says
I'm more likely to discover a living dragon
than a bird that hungry people ate
because it was big, and women plucked
because bright feathers looked pretty
when used as fluttering decorations
for fancy hats, a bird that lost its habitat
when forests were chopped down
to plant sugarcane.

That's all it takes to wipe out a species.
Just a few ordinary people making a string
of greedy
decisions.

Silenced

~ LUZA ~

The extinct Cuban macaw was mostly
a red bird, with a sun-hued splash of gold
on the back of its neck, green-blue wings,
and a purple fringe on the rump. . . .

Yes, that intelligent species, *Ara tricolor*,
just might have been the most beautiful bird,
and now it's gone.
Forever.

Abuelo's tears look like stars
in a moonless sky, the brightness
an unimaginable number of light-years
away.

On Patrol
∽ EDVER ∽

I'll never go back to that museum room.
From now on, I want to be out in the forest
with Dad, riding little Platero
beside tall Rocinante.

Even on a small pony, I feel
big, *grande*,
strong,
a wildlife
conservation
superhero
in training!

When I go back to Miami in September,
I'll start studying hard, learning everything
I can manage, just to make sure I get into college
and become a specialist. One of the ologies
would probably be best: ornithology for birds,
entomology for insects, herpetology—reptiles,
mammalogy—mammals, ichthyology—fish . . .
there's no end to the variety of animals
I could rescue from poachers, hunters,
and other creepy losers.

In the meantime, if any of those sorts
of selfish people show up here

in *my* family's forest, I'll make sure
I'm ready and waiting, just like Dad
with his fake gun, only I'll think up new ways
to scare bad guys away—I'll turn it into
a clever game, roar like a dragon,
spit out a waterfall
of flames!

It's never too early to start working
toward a goal, so I throw myself into the effort
to learn from Dad, following him around
with lots of questions, writing down
the answers, and studying everything
he says, just to prove
my enthusiasm.

It works!
Dad tells me he thinks I'll be heroic
someday.

Waiting, Waiting, Waiting
~ LUZA ~

Papi seems to prefer Edver,
but I know it's just because they've never
had a chance to work together
like a team.

With the words NEW *PAPILIO* deleted,
I have no way to lure Mamá here,
so there's nothing to do but *resolver*,
solve problems,
inventar, invent.

Otherwise, she and I will never
know mother-daughter tears, laughter,
or any more ordinary form
of teamwork.

So where do I start?
What should I make?

I remember how hard Abuelo worked
to teach me English, even though he only
knew what he'd learned in college
a long time ago, and I was so bored
that I barely paid attention.
Now, his patience is exactly
the kind of perseverance I need,

but in the meantime, all we do is watch
our blurry TV, all the telenovelas that bring
waves of joy and tears.

Then, during an interruption for news,
we see a Miami poet reading miraculous verses
as the US Embassy finally reopens
right across from our seawall!

More than half a century of anger
between enemy countries
has suddenly been replaced
by the flow of rhythmic words.

Will Mamá and I ever
have our own chance
to talk to each other
and make peace?

Thrills
~ EDVER ~

Patrolling with Dad, and the renewal
of diplomatic relations
are both exciting,
and so is a baby *jutía*
that I find in the forest,
my chance to rescue one
little individual
if not a whole species.

Suddenly, my entire life is a rush of duties—
feeding, brushing, cleaning, until after
a few hardworking weeks,
the funny creature is able
to sit on my lap
and eat from a spoon,
looking as silly
as a cross between a beaver
and a cartoon.

So I name him Snoopy.
If Abuelo can have a wiener dog
called Jutía, then I can name my real *jutía*
after a beagle!

He's as mischievous as a monkey,
climbing up to open cupboards

and empty bags of precious rationed rice,
sacks of coffee, and tins of homegrown spices—
saffron, nutmeg, coriander, so that the kitchen
smells like a mixture of pumpkin pie
and curry.

Snoopy helps me laugh out loud
at least fifty times each day, but he also
makes me work so hard that I feel
like a full-time zookeeper,
superskilled
and useful!

When I hoe weeds in the garden,
Snoopy rides on my shoulder,
and every time I ride down to the village,
he's right there with me, like a little brother.

Is this the way Mom felt when she took me away?
Responsible, constantly ready to help?
Was Luza left behind only because she
was one year older, able to run around
instead of clinging?

That would make sense.
I could understand anyone's
lack of confidence
in a small
boat

on a huge
ocean.

I'm glad I don't remember
the size
of those
waves. . . .

My Shrinking World

~ LUZA ~

I used to think life was enormous,
but now
it seems tiny and dull.

My heart is like a frozen zoo,
the last cells of a vanishing species
preserved with ice, just in case someday
there's a way to bring lost treasures
back to life.

Feeling vicious, I show my brother
a photo album with pictures of Abuela,
the mother our mamá lost only last year,
without ever coming back to visit
even once
to say good-bye.

Edver could have met her, if our two countries
and our divided family had been normal.

Red, blue, green, yellow, purple,
all the shimmering colors
of an extinct Cuban macaw,
that's how complicated
my thoughts seem now,
inside this private freezer,
my secret mind.

Communication

~ EDVER ~

When two snail mail letters from Mom
arrive with colorful Fijian stamps, I feel wide,
then narrow, and in the end, I go back
to feeling mixed up.

Nothing but questions.
How are you and Abuelo,
your sister, Yoel, the forest?

Not a single answer.
No explanations,
Just an ordinary hurricane
of Mom-powered
confusion.

No return address, no way to respond.
If I could send my complicated mother
a simple letter right now,
what would I say?

Maybe the first thing I should be asking is
if that injured bicyclist is completely okay,
but all I actually want to know is why
can't Mom and I both go back and forth
between two homes,
our city world
and this forest?

What's the use though—my mother never
really answers my questions about Cuba.
She still calls Dad Yoel, as if she wants me
to think of him as a stranger, not family,
just a name,
not a relationship.

When I was little,
the first ten thousand times
I asked if I had a father,
she just shrugged.
Then, when I was big enough to know better,
she admitted, *se quedó*, he stayed.
It's a phrase every Cuban in Miami
understands.

Now, all she ever says is how complicated
everything is, and how someday
I'll understand, when I'm older
and wiser.

But she doesn't seem all that wise either.
First she abandons Luza,
then she leaves me
with babysitters while she travels,
and now she can't even offer
a sensible explanation
of anything
that matters.

So when Snoopy starts chewing up
that airmail envelope from Fiji, I let him
just go ahead and destroy it completely.

Later, while Luza silently reads her letter,
I pretend I don't know what she's doing.
That way, we can both act like we're
still alone in our shared confusion.

Trying to understand grown-ups
is one of life's greatest scientific
puzzles.

First Contact

~ LUZA ~

Descriptions.
The people, houses, flora, fauna,
and beaches of Fiji.

Endemics.
All the rare Lazarus species of islands.
Isolation.
Separation.

Lo siento, I'm sorry.
Perdóname, forgive me.
Por favor, please.

I feel like a shoreline absorbing
the first view of an approaching
tsunami.

With no return address, I can't answer,
but if I could, maybe I'd just send
an empty envelope.

It wouldn't be the first time
I sought papery vengeance.

Over the years, I've imagined
mailing nothingness

to Miami
over
and over
like a migration
of resentments.

Now, when my brother asks, I say that Papi
stayed here to guard our forest, keeping
evil poachers away.

But Edver assures me that our mother left
to do the same thing, except that she tries
to protect the whole world's wildlife, not just
one small jungle refuge.

Separate, our parents are like two planets
orbiting the sun, their paths never meeting.
Together, they could have been
a heroic team.

This Brother-Sister Mess

Our shared maze of disappointment
brings us closer again.

We agree that we need to go out
and *resolver*
by inventing adventures.

So we follow the waterfall trail,
comforted
by the reaching arms of trees.

Then the strangest thing happens,
the worst sort of weirdness, an event
so unbelievable that it has to be real,
because everyone knows that true life
is always more bizarre than fairy tales.

The first sign of an intruder in our forest
is a cleverly disguised campsite,
almost completely hidden by tree ferns.

The camouflaged campsite is eerie.
Butterfly nets, kill jars, a stranger.
The stranger—yes, that exact same man
from Mom's photos, the creep with a face
that looked too big in his bad selfies.

Now his features have shrunk down
to their normal size, but what's he doing here
in our world of ferns, palms, ceibas, and wild figs,
armed with all that suspicious insect-collecting
equipment?

Snoopy perches on my shoulder, pulling
at my ears, cheerfully unaware that I'm boiling
with fury.

Niños, the creep says, calling out to me and Luza.
Trabajo, he invites, offering work as he tries
to hand us nets, along with jars that stink
like mothballs.

My sister glances at me, looking so worried
that I'm afraid she'll say something, but instead
she turns and races away, so I pull Snoopy off
my shoulders, hug him in my arms,
and run, stumbling as I go,
without answering
any of the creep's
surprised
shouts.

What a disaster.

This is our fault!
We brought him here
by trying to lure Mom.

But what if she's with him?
Isn't that a possibility?
She's probably back there
in the tent, asleep or too lazy
to come out and greet us. . . .

Suspicious
~ LUZA ~

We go back the next day,
just to make sure Mamá isn't here,
ready to visit.

But she's nowhere to be found,
even though we try all sorts of fancy tricks,
taking turns distracting the insect collector
long enough for each of us to peer
into that tent, searching for a woman's
clothes, shoes, footprints. . . .

The collector doesn't tell us his name,
but when he repeats his offer to pay
for specimens, we agree, just to see
if playing along with him will lead
to more information.

Quest
～ EDVER ～

Nothing makes sense.
How did a guy who knows Mom
end up on territory patrolled by Dad?
Why would he dare to come here
and kill creatures that are protected
by the ex-husband of the scientist
he's dating?

Or have we missed something?
What else could there be?
Maybe it's all really simple.
Just friends,
not a couple!
Someone Dad knows,
a collector who has permission?
No, I don't even begin to believe
any of my made-up stories.
None of it rings true.
I need facts if I'm ever going to be
a real scientist.

Worse Than We Imagined
~ LUZA ~

As soon as we have a chance to go back
to Yavi's computer, the ugliness
becomes ominous.

My brother searches and searches
until he discovers the most evil level
of greed.

El novio de Mamá has his own
rare insect auction site.

We find his photo, next to an ad
offering the "world's most unique
Caribbean island *Papilio*,
details on request,
$100,000 starting bid."

Disgusting

All the other auction prices
are just as grotesque.

Hercules beetles, the strongest animals
on Earth, bombardier beetles that spray
stinky goo, a praying mantis that mimics
a purple orchid, another one that looks
like soft green moss, and a Queen Alexandra's birdwing,
the world's largest birdwing butterfly,
all the way from Papua New Guinea,
wingspan one foot wide,
males blue and green
with gold abdomens,
females a little smaller,
chocolate brown and cream
with furry red tufts
on the thorax.

I wish I couldn't read.
It would be heaven to remain unaware
of this catastrophe that I created
by teaching my clueless sister
how to type lies on a keyboard.

It's easy to see that Mom's creepy friend
is a criminal, because his spectacular photo

of a tiger swallowtail butterfly
is the Traveler, a Jamaican *Papilio*
that sometimes wanders
onto Cuban territory, blown
off course by wind.

I recognize all the details of the species
from Abuelo's lessons in his museum room.

The Traveler is one of the highest-flying insects
on Earth, almost as strong as a bird, but definitely
not new
to science.

Using its photo must just be a way to tempt
inexperienced new collectors, the ones
with plenty of money but not enough
knowledge to realize that the smuggler
hasn't caught his valuable prize yet.

That's why he's here.
To catch our fake insect
and sell it for a fortune.

I don't know how Mom
fits into his plan,

but I'm pretty sure
she wouldn't
go along with it
if she knew.

Too bad she's so emotionally clueless
that he fooled her.

Now I Know
~ LUZA ~

So this is how it feels
to be the sorry one.

Has Mamá been wandering around
all these years
swayed by powerful waves
of regret?

Abuelo and Dad would hate me if they knew
how recklessly Edver and I tried to cheat reality
by telling a lie that turned us
into tricked fools
not tricksters.

Horrified
~ EDVER ~

The creep has altered his labels
to look old, with dates that make the Traveler
seem to have been collected before 1973,
when 175 countries approved a treaty
called CITES, the Convention on International
Trade in Endangered Species of Flora and Fauna.

Anything collected before CITES existed
can be sold as an antique, a curiosity,
not a crime.

Mom always says that if CITES had been passed
a couple of centuries earlier, there might still be
Tasmanian tigers, Barbary lions, Steller's sea cows,
Carolina parakeets, dodo birds, great auks,
and passenger pigeons.

I don't know which part of the mess we created
is scarier: the way Luza and I posted a few words
for just a couple of minutes and ended up
inviting a monster into our forest, or the way
Mom has somehow managed to get fooled
into accepting a criminal as her boyfriend.

Maybe no one else on Earth knows exactly
how slimy this auction guy is—probably

my sister and I are the only witnesses
to a crime in progress. . . .

Could we catch him and turn him over
to the authorities, becoming
wildlife protection superheroes,
instead of troublemakers?

Our pictures might be on TV!
Snoopy would wave from my shoulder,
and all those kids at school who call me a nerd
would suddenly realize that being smart
can't hurt.

Bizarre
~ LUZA ~

During the hours we spend debating
possible strategies, strange things happen,
just like every year at this time,
when big black-and-orange land crabs
march through the village, clacking
noisy claws as they migrate
from our mountains down to the coast
where they'll deposit eggs
in rocky tide pools.

Nothing can stop the crabs.
They never turn back, not even when women
grab them and pile them—stomping and snapping—
into buckets, planning delicious meals
even though the crabs keep climbing out
and walking away.

Tourists come to watch.
Grinning foreigners rush around,
handing out gifts—pencils for some children,
baseballs for others, T-shirts for most,
but not all.

The result is a near riot
by mothers who want
all the gifts for every child,

so that pretty soon
blue-uniformed police
and green-clad soldiers
have to break up the scuffles,
and everyone goes home miserable,
furious with their neighbors
and disgusted by the strangers,
who don't seem capable
of understanding
poverty.

When the ugly uproar is finally over,
Edver and I return to Yavi's computer,
relieved that he doesn't seem to mind
sharing, and his sweet old *bisabuela*
barely notices us, because she's so busy
boiling
land crabs.

Searching for Secrets
~ EDVER ~

Buried deep in the belly of the computer's
information junkyard, I find scraps to help
solve our mystery—the smuggler's nickname,
his real name, and worst of all,
his prison record.

He's called the Human Vacuum Cleaner.
Once, he was arrested with half a million
rare butterflies, dead and dusty,
spread all over his otherwise
ordinary house in California.

He has a shop in Japan, too, where he sells
live rhinoceros beetles in vending machines.
They're prized by people who keep
the giant insects as pets, setting up matches
to watch them sword fight with their sharp horns.

But Mom's disgusting boyfriend
doesn't just sell bugs—he's been caught smuggling
parrots, macaws, cockatoos, aquarium fish,
ghost orchids,
paintings, and statues.

He's not even a scientist,
just a businessman,

making money
any way he can.

I bet he hires children to help him
wherever he goes.

It's easy to imagine him camped out
in other jungles, waiting for poor kids
to come along—hungry ones who need
a few coins for buying dinner
more than they need to know
whether the animals they kill
might be the last living
individuals
on Earth.

Whole species have been destroyed
by the Human Vacuum Cleaner's
greediness.

Strange World
~ LUZA ~

I've never lived away from our forest,
so it's hard for me to understand any place
where such a monster of slaughter can serve
only twenty-one months in prison.

His specialty is finishing off the last living members
of rare species, in order to make the price
of dead specimens
skyrocket.

He even keeps greenhouses
for rearing endangered plants and animals,
just so he can sell them to collectors
at some horrible moment in the future
when all the wild ones
are gone.

Now that we know who he is
and what he does, my brother and I
are more confused than ever.

If we tell Papi and Abuelo, they might be able
to catch him, but will they ever trust us again?
Shouldn't we try to keep our mistake secret
and solve this problem on our own,
inventing some way to pretend

that it's not all
our fault?

If only I could time travel
back to one minute before I learned how
to spread a single, tiny, dangerous lie!

Those two words, NEW *PAPILIO*,
flew so far across the infinite Internet
that they will never completely
disappear.

I can't resolve or invent the past.
I need a way to change the future.

Storm!

~ EDVER ~

While we're wrapped up in our struggle
to make a decision, rain and thunder
finally arrive, ending the drought
that seemed endless.

Maybe the Human Vacuum Cleaner
will get flooded out, pick up his tent,
and abandon his dream of selling
each example of a new *Papilio*
for one hundred thousand dollars
or more.

But no.
He's still there, we check quickly,
hiding carefully before sneaking
back to our house
to make plans.

The question we keep asking each other
is why hasn't our dad found the smuggler
and arrested him?

He barely seems to patrol these days.
All he does is sit around with Abuelo,
both of them nodding and murmuring
as they sort messy papers

in the museum room,
as if they're wrapped up
in their own
secret plan.

I've just started getting to know my father,
and now I already miss him, as if summer
has ended, and I'm on my way home.

But I'm not.
There's still time
for surprises.

After the Rain

Tree frogs, birdsongs,
sighing mud,
and thousands
of butterflies
puddling.

Iguanas sunbathe on our roof.
A *majá* snake coils itself around a branch.
Chickens chuckle, and a blue Cinderella lizard
lifts its delicately
clinging feet
one by one.

My long-lost brother has turned out to be
such a mixture of trouble and friendship!

What should we scheme together?
How should we act?

I can't bear the thought of revealing
our shared disaster
to Papi and Abuelo . . .
but we can't ignore the smuggler, either,
because together, Edver and I hold the fate
of so many fragile, fluttering lives
in our guilty hands.

Keys

~ EDVER ~

The downpour gives way to heat.
In the village, there are rumors
of public parks with suddenly legal
Internet access
all over the island,
a change that could bring
normal communication, maybe even
modern video games, but I don't have my phone
and even if I did, I'm not sure those dragon flames
would mean as much to me anymore,
now that I'm stranded in the middle
of a real-life catastrophe.

I need weapons, and a plan—maybe steal
Dad's fake rifle, and hope to scare the
Human Vacuum Cleaner
into surrendering?

Or catch a poisonous scorpion
and sneak it into the creepy dude's tent?
Or convince him that blue-clad police
and green-uniformed soldiers
are already on their way to arrest him?

Mom taught me to make decisions
by following a series of choices

patterned after the scientific keys
found in every field guide
for identifying animals.

Six legs or eight?
Three body parts or two?
Often winged, never winged?
May have chewing mouthparts,
or always found with piercing mouths?

In this case, the only two answers
are insects or spiders, but other keys
are a lot more complicated, with pairs
of choices
that go on and on
until you can finally
reach the end,
and identify
any mysterious
specimen.

Emotional choices aren't as easy,
but the basic method still works.

Right or wrong?
Fair or unjust?
Resulting in peace of mind
or guilt?
All you have to do is write your own

scientific key for sorting out the general
confusion.

But Luza and I don't do it the easy way.
Instead, we keep debating possibilities
until we're so exhausted that she falls asleep
in a hammock out in the garden, while I play
with Snoopy as if I'm still an innocent
little kid who doesn't need to make
any huge, world-changing
decisions.

Stalling for Time

~ LUZA ~

I only pretend
to be peacefully sleeping
while my brother's mind
rushes off in search
of trouble,
his specialty.

I wish that we could splash truth
all over our lives, like paint or glue
spilled from a broken bottle
while making a mosaic.

All we would have to do is clean up
and start over again, but instead,
here we are, facing a dilemma every bit
as challenging as negotiations
between enemy nations.

Sneaking Away
~ EDVER ~

I can't wait for Luza to wake up, so I go off alone
with Snoopy huddled under my sweaty shirt.

I keep expecting someone to stop me,
but Dad and Abuelo are both busy sorting papers
and using the microscope to identify an enormous
metallic green, robot-armored jewel beetle.

They're so absorbed in their work
that they don't even look up once,
no matter how many times I try
to make myself visible
by hovering near windows.

If only I could click a dot on a screen,
end this part of my life
and start over.

Adrenalin must be filling my brain with light,
because everything looks both bright
and blurry at the same time, like trees
seen through a kaleidoscope
of broken colors.

Snoopy scratches my chest
with his sharp little claws, so I pull him out,

set him on my shoulder, and ask myself
where I'm supposed to find the courage
to confront the world's MOST WANTED
wildlife smuggler.

Then I recognize the truth.
I can't do this alone.
I need help
from my sister
and her weird ideas, all that magic realism,
her own special, strange style of art
with illusions clever enough to fool
a trickster.

So I turn back and run until I reach Luza
and shake her awake—even though
now I can tell that she was faking—and then
quickly, I explain my hastily imagined plan,
maybe a bit too loudly.
I hope Dad and Abuelo didn't
hear me.

The Challenge

Ilusión can mean illusion or dream,
the wild fantasy of someday reaching
a goal, but where do I start?

My brother's odd scheme
actually makes sense.

Paper, *por supuesto*, of course,
sí, *sí*, yes, yes, I have plenty of sheets
that I made myself, as soft and flexible
as cloth, crafted by soaking newspapers,
then rinsing them in our old Russian
washing machine, filtering roughness
through a screen, hanging the paper
up to dry, and finally, dying each sheet
with a color found only in nature,
so that whenever I want to make
a collage, I have plenty of dazzling,
softly glowing choices.

Yellow from saffron, pink from lichens,
the surprising green of red onion skins,
and a blue so deep that it looks like night,
a color yielded by boiling indigo leaves
until the sky-hued dye is almost black.

Saffron and indigo sheets are all we need.
Yellow wings, cave-dark body, antennae,
and head, an illusion of both sorts,
the dream
and this trick,
almost magic,
yet at the same time
so convincing
that my NEW *PAPILIO*
looks completely
real.

Kill Jar
～ EDVER ～

Inside a glass bottle,
the paper butterfly looks amazing.
Those wings actually flutter!
If my sister's masterpiece
weren't so perfect, I'd call it gross,
cool, awesome, all the words I used for death
way back at the beginning of summer
when I still thought killing was something
that only happened on a screen, where it was
temporary and harmless, just one more
scientific skill.

Now, inside that kill jar, stinky mothballs
really seem to be doing their deadly job,
filling the air with poison, so the striped
paper wings
look like they're suffering
slowly.

Danger
~ LUZA ~

We have a fake butterfly,
but we need a good story,
the right words to trick
a trickster.

Above us, branches, leaves, and sky
seem to cheer our daring scheme.

I have handcuffs I crafted from scraps
of stiff plastic trash, hard water bottles
left on the trail by tourists.

I also have a glass jar containing
my homemade magic, the spirit
of a butterfly, captured
on paper.

Preparation
~ EDVER ~

All I have is Snoopy and courage.
If this were a game, there would be
so many possibilities—weapons, elixirs,
precious gems to trade, cave-dwelling
secrets
to discover. . . .

But it's not a game, and if we die
there won't be any way to start over.

So we need the best story we can invent,
something believable and astonishing
at the same time, both ordinary
and thrilling, a temptation,
a magnet, a lure. . . .

As soon as we find the creep's campsite—
peaceful, surrounded by tree ferns, magnolias,
and towering palms, Luza begins telling him
her newly invented tale, twisting her voice
into torches
of fascination, each strand
as bright as a leaping flame
in a prehistoric fire,
with a whole village

gathered around,
listening.

But it's just him, one ugly-minded smuggler,
a man so mean and greedy, he'd probably sell
his own relatives, if someone wealthy
wanted to collect them.

Only the comforting silence
of curling fern leaves
keeps me calm enough
to resist
screaming.

Confrontation

~ LUZA ~

The Human Vacuum Cleaner's interest grows
as he hears my claim that my brother's little pet
is new to science,
a natural hybrid
between coastal *jutías*
and the mountain form,
a cuddly creature, just as friendly
and intelligent as a dog,
but small and cute,
the perfect gift for any rich foreign child
who deserves
a rare treasure.

Yes, I've captured his attention, and now
all I have to do is hold my fake butterfly
close enough to be noticed, but not so near
that he'll see glued strips of soft paper
instead of a valuable, endangered
tiger swallowtail.

So while my brother uses Snoopy
as a hook to reel in the smuggler,
I flit around his cluttered campsite,
my fake kill jar visible,
the makeshift handcuffs
safely hidden.

Five American dollars.
That's what the monster-man offers me
for this jar and its enticing contents,
five dollars for a butterfly
he plans to auction for more than
one hundred thousand dollars.

Claro que sí, I answer, yes, of course,
still keeping the prize out of range,
away from his hands,
letting him spin around,
trying to follow me as I perform a silly,
childish dance, pretending to celebrate
the fortune I've just been offered,
because five American *dólares*
in our remote forest
is like a thousand dollars anywhere else
on Earth—no wonder so many poor people
sell wildlife!

The Human Vacuum Cleaner's ugly eyes
watch me intently, as if he plans to grab the jar
and race away with my NEW *PAPILIO*,
instead of paying me the amount he just
promised.

He must think I'm stupid!
Is this how he fooled Mamá
into liking, or loving, or worse—

could they already
be married?

Is he my brother's new
stepfather?

Battle

How quickly a victory turns toward failure.
The smuggler grabs Snoopy with one hand,
pushes me down with the other, and rushes
toward my sister, who still holds the jar
just out of reach.

Snoopy squeals, scratching
the guy's neck so hard that I see
streaks of blood, hear a curse
followed by a moan, proof
that my brave pet's claws
really hurt.

My sister darts and dodges,
her soccer skills incredibly useful
for avoiding those grasping fingers.

The only thing I know how to do is skate,
so I get up and slide around on the soggy slope,
kicking up a slimy wet mess so I can thrash
the creep's face with blinding mud.

When he trips and falls to his knees,
I rescue Snoopy while Luza clamps
those flimsy-looking plastic handcuffs
onto the Human Vacuum Cleaner's wrists

and yanks them tight, catching him off guard
as he tries to scrub
rough soil
from his eyes
with trapped fists.

We won!
Now what?

Somehow, we have to stop him from running,
but it's already too late, he's up and sprinting,
bound hands not enough to keep him still.

If only we'd thought of extra cuffs
for his feet.

Battlefield

~ LUZA ~

I've seen enough fights at school to know
that winning one round isn't enough
to end the pummeling, especially
when your enemy gets away.

So I run after him, shrieking to startle
all the hidden forest creatures, hoping a flock
of noisy parrots might rise from the trees,
so alarmed that their racket of squawks
will make this horrible man hesitate
just long enough
to be caught.

But then what?
Once again, we didn't think ahead.
We're no wiser than we were when I sent
those two words, NEW *PAPILIO*, hurtling
across a vast, eerie, man-made universe—
the Internet.

Whirl!

~ EDVER ~

With Snoopy clinging to my hair
and Luza swooping ahead of me,
I feel like a useless little kid,
only one year younger
than my sister, but a lot less
athletic, so I go back to trying
my usual skills, sliding and thinking
at the same time, picturing a game
with all these players—towering tree ferns
a great background for any display
of dragon flames . . .

only I don't really know how to breathe fire,
and Snoopy is practically pulling my ears off,
with Luza falling behind as the smuggler
rushes ahead, straight into a storm of shouts,
cries, whoops, and pounding hooves,
all the noises I've heard so often
as two armies of electronic knights
gallop straight toward each other
right before clashing.

This time, instead of swords and lances,
the only weapons are looped ropes,
twirling lassos aimed by Dad, Abuelo,
and a bunch of other old folks.

My brain feels like it's oozing
in slow motion, while my body rolls—
dreamlike—the pain of crashing
softened by mud, Snoopy kept safe
by his own acrobatics,
and Luza far ahead now,
almost as distant
as those nooses
that tighten around
the shoulders and hips
of the Human Vacuum Cleaner,
a real-life evil villain
defeated by two kids,
one *jutía*, and a cheering crowd
of white-haired wizards
on horseback.

Los abuelos must have learned
how to swing rodeo ropes
way back in the middle
of the twentieth century
when they were young
and this mountain
was still surrounded
by ranches with cowboys.

Well, cowgirls, too, I guess,
because some of those old ladies
sure look
like experts.

Triumph!

Instead of a criminal, the poacher
now looks more like a caterpillar, wrapped up
in so many layers of lassos that he seems
to be snugly tucked into a cocoon
of tangled ropes.

Oímos, Abuelo says.
We heard.

Increíble, Papi adds.
Incredible.

I can't tell what they heard,
or whether our father means
that we're unbelievable in a foolish way
or an amazing one . . .

but who cares,
because Edver, Snoopy, and I are all safe,
and one of the world's worst poachers
is on his way to prison.

Summer's End
~ EDVER ~

Explaining everything to Dad
is punishment enough to last
a lifetime.

Confessions aren't easy.
I'd give anything to avoid describing
the way I guided my sister's disastrous
message, the first words she ever wrote
on any computer.

But what follows is so weird
that even an island without Internet
begins to seem normal.

Mom shows up.
Mom and a man she introduces
as a United States Fish and Wildlife agent,
operating undercover
to help her catch
a notorious smuggler.

The wildlife cop is a muscular guy
with blue eyes that are directed too often
at my mother, and too nervously
toward my father.

Poor Dad.
He looks furious and sorrowful
at the same time.

Poor Mom.
She's so shocked when she finds out
that we already took care of the bad guy,
and all she can do is apologize for being late.
She makes excuses—the car they rented in Havana
broke down, they had to hitchhike
just like everyone else, their rides
were slow and clunky. . . .

Poor Luza.
She looks stunned.

Abuelo is the only one who seems ready
to hug his daughter, welcome her back,
and treat her like part of this crazy, mixed-up,
two-country, disaster-attracting family.

Reappearance
～ LUZA ～

I can't believe Mamá is here now,
even though for so long I hoped
she would arrive.

She looks just like her photos,
but her expression is so gentle,
as if she's suddenly
human.

Hugs, embraces, apologies, explanations,
and yet there's this distance, the effect of so many
unchangeable years apart.
How can ninety simple miles
of ordinary, rolling blue ocean
keep so many families divided
until now?

Each thought is a wave that sweeps over me,
tasting as salty
as tears.

Dizzy
~ EDVER ~

Earth rotates on its axis,
orbits around the sun,
and glides along with
the whole solar system
zooming through
our galaxy.

All those light-years
might as well be a fantasy,
because reality and myths
feel the same now.

Mom claims she knew nothing
about the Human Vacuum Cleaner
until she was already dating him,
and noticed how unnaturally fascinated
he became when he saw Luza's note
about a new species of *Papilio*.

So she rushed some quick research,
just like I did, by matching his photo
to insect auction sites, and figuring out
all his dangerous lies.

Then she helped international authorities
set up a sting, only they didn't arrive

in time, and everything was left up to
the locals here on our mountain.

She still seems surprised
that we managed just fine.

Now she has a much harder task,
trying to find Luza's forgiveness
for our family's sliced-in-half
past.

Listening
~ LUZA ~

Mamá says she left me
only because I was so attached to Papi,
and because she was afraid I'd fall off
her little stolen boat, and because
she was too cowardly to wait
until both my baby brother and I
were older, before seeking
her own chance to establish
an internationally
successful career
with limitless
freedom to travel.

Abuelo stayed to help me, she adds,
and Abuela was still alive back then,
so they faithfully stayed in touch,
always making plans
to be reunited
someday.

Everyone wrote letters at first, the old way,
on paper, but because the US and Cuba
were enemies with no direct mail service,
envelopes had to travel in and out
of other countries, often getting lost
along the way.

It was a challenge.
No es fácil. It's not easy.
Mamá lost her ability to *resolver*.
She gave up trying to solve problems.
Now she's right here in front of me,
telling stories along with a wildlife policeman,
both of them turning back and forth
to see if Papi and Abuelo
still have anything else
to say.

They don't.
Neither does Edver.

I'm the only one with an infinite supply
of riddles that burst from my heart
leaving shards
of question marks
all over our forest floor,
ready to be pieced together
into a delicate,
fluttering,
fragile
family mosaic.

Hearing

Research teams.
International cooperation.
That's what the forms Dad
was supposed to fill out
were all about.

UNESCO. The United Nations.
Designation as a world Biosphere Reserve.
A wildlife survey that will bring researchers
of all sorts.

Tree roots must be growing right into my brain,
because somehow I manage to sit still and gather up
all the mud, sludge, mold, slime, grime,
and crusty, old leftover feelings
as they're finally
revealed.

Between the Trees

~ LUZA ~

I look up.
An extravaganza
of light
and shadow!

I look down.
The treasure of soil
and moisture!

In between,
so many individual branches,
this harmony of roots
and wings, a whole world
of possibilities.

Family Magic

If this were a video game,
I'd wipe out the whole bunch of us
and start over,
knowing exactly what
to expect.

Only I wouldn't know, not really,
because tomorrow
will probably be
just as weird.

So I listen to plans for Snoopy to stay here
and be cared for by Abuelo, while Luza
and I each go back to our own schools.

There are other plans too, for Abuelo
and my sister to stay with us at Christmas,
and then Mom will bring me back here
during spring break, and maybe again
next summer. . . .

While Mom and Dad talk to everyone else
except each other,
I try to hear any sort
of hope for this Lazarus family's
crazy future.

Together?
Separate?
Back and forth?

I could write *THE END*
but it wouldn't be true,
because our lost-and-found
two-country story
finally seems ready
to start over.

The future is huge.
There's still plenty of time
for surprises.

Acknowledgments

I thank God for biodiversity and the people who work to protect endangered species and threatened habitats. I'm profoundly grateful to my husband, entomologist Curtis Engle, for traveling with me to some of Cuba's spectacular UNESCO World Network of Biosphere Reserves. Special thanks to my relatives in Cuba for their hospitality.

For information about the worst Human Vacuum Cleaner, I'm indebted to entomologist Lynn LeBeck, who recommended *Winged Obsession: The Pursuit of the World's Most Notorious Butterfly Smuggler*, by Jessica Speart. Special thanks to entomologist Mike Klein for confirming the presence of jewel-like beetles in Cuba.

For ongoing encouragement, I wish to thank Jennifer Crow and Kristene Scholefield of the Arne Nixon Center for the Study of Children's Literature, and friends Sandra Ríos Balderrama, Joan Schoettler, and Angelica Carpenter. Special thanks to my wonderful agent, Michelle Humphrey; my incredible editor, Reka Simonsen; and the entire amazing Atheneum/Simon & Schuster publishing team.

Truly Cool Biodiversity Words

Biodiversity: Biological diversity; in other words, the world's great variety of plant and animal species. Some of the most biodiverse areas on Earth are tropical rain forests.

Endemic Species: Plants or animals found only in a particular area. Due to isolation, many islands have endemic species found nowhere else on Earth.

Lazarus Species: Plants or animals that are thought to be extinct, until they're found alive. Some Lazarus species, such as the Cuban solenodon, were classified as extinct for less than a century before being rediscovered. Others were known only from fossils until living specimens were identified. An example is el Monito del Monte, a miniature marsupial thought to have been extinct for eleven million years before one was found alive in a bamboo thicket in Chile.

World Network of Biosphere Reserves: A network of biodiverse areas designated by UNESCO, a branch of the United Nations. By 2016 there were close to seven hundred world Biosphere Reserves on Earth, including six in Cuba. Some of these protected areas cross borders, uniting countries with a common wildlife conservation goal. Others are isolated. Many include local farms and villages where people make a living by using natural resources wisely, instead of recklessly. To learn more about these communities, visit unesco.org.

Truly Uncool, Creepy People

Real-Life Human Vacuum Cleaners who kill endangered species just to sell them to collectors. In the most horrifying cases, they kill and hoard the last members of a species in order to charge higher prices as soon as they become extinct.

Turn the page for a sneak peek at

Lion Island

MARGARITA ENGLE

Lion Island

CUBA'S WARRIOR
OF WORDS

Running with Words

ANTONIO CHUFFAT
Age 12

Year of the Goat
1871

Carrying Words

The arrival of *los californios*
changed everything.
School.
Work.
Hope.
All are mine, now that I have a job
delivering mysterious messages
for Señor Tung Kong Lam from Shanghai,
who fled to Cuba after only one year
in San Francisco.

California's violence must be dragon-fierce
to make so many refugees seek new homes
on this island
of war.

Shaped by Words

My ancestors were born
in Asia, Africa, and Europe,
but sometimes I feel like a bird
that has migrated across the vast ocean
to this one
small island,
as if I am
shrinking.

I don't know my *africana* mother's language.
I hardly even know her enslaved relatives.
I only know the *chino* half of my family.

Teachers call me a child of three worlds,
but I feel like a creature of three words:
Freedom.
Liberty.
Hope.

Craving Words

I was terrified when my father
brought me to this busy city of La Habana
from our quiet village.

He left me alone at a school
called *el Colegio para Desamparados
de la Raza de Color—*
the School for Unprotected Ones
of the Race of Color—
where I am only one of many
part-African children.

Most are orphans, abandoned, unwanted,
cast out like trash,
but I am here only because
my father wants me to learn proper Spanish
instead of blending it with his native language,
the Cantonese of southern China,
a huge country that I've never seen
and can barely imagine,
so accustomed am I
to this small island's
mixture
of thoughts
and tongues.

Lion Men, Peacock Men,
a Battle of Words

The messages I carry for Señor Lam
go to businessmen, diplomats, and soldiers
from two empires.

Spain's soldiers are familiar to me,
but until so recently, I lived in the little village
of Jovellanos, where I never saw imperial China's
regal visitors.

Military leaders from Peking wear sleek golden lions
embroidered on their chests like roaring hearts.

Soldiers of lower rank are marked by tigers, panthers,
or leopards.

But the most powerful symbols belong to diplomats—
men of words, whose silk robes are embroidered
with shimmering peacocks, long-legged storks,
or graceful
white herons.

Even a button can have meaning.
Red, pink, blue, clear crystal, brown clay.
Each hue grants a diplomat
the authority to settle
certain types
of arguments.

Whenever I hover in the corner of a fancy room,
awaiting a written reply that I can carry back
to my busy employer, I notice the way soldiers
always yield to civil officials.

These peacock-decorated peacemakers
are more respected
than growling-lion
military heroes.

Dream Words

When I close my eyes late at night
after school and work,
the comfort of sleep
does not
find me.

All I see is a dreamlike parade of beasts,
snarling and shrieking,
while dignified winged beings
quietly explain their POWERFUL
opinions.

Will anyone ever
listen
to me?

What would I say if they did?
Will I grow up to be a roaring lion-soldier
or a calmly speaking
diplomat-bird?

Weapon Words

POWER is a word that binds me in its spell
of fiery strength.

POWER allows Spain to rule Cuba.
POWER keeps *africano* slaves
and indentured *chinos*
in chains.

But I am free-born, working, studying,
and listening to Señor Lam
as he speaks of democracy. . . .

One man,
one vote!

Imagine having choices
instead of
FEARS.

Words Are Possibilities

During mornings at school, I recite Spanish
verb forms, but my afternoons are spent racing
with urgent notes written in Chinese characters.

Each message wrapped
in the warmth of my hand
feels alive.

Some are letters to the editors of newspapers
in Shanghai or Peking, and I am the one who runs
with feet that pound like drums
on slippery wooden walkways,
pummeled by rain that feels
like a hammer, driving ideas
into my mind.

Translation, understanding, an exchange
of meanings . . .
Could I ever be a patient diplomat, or would I prefer
the adventurous life of a lion?

Written Words

Señor Lam tells me that I would be
a good newspaper reporter,
the way I always
watch
listen,
learn,
before opening
my diary
to write.

Disturbing Words

Running, I pass slaves tied to whipping posts,
slaves chained to each other, slaves shackled
to wagons. . . .

Then I enter a neighborhood of *chinos*,
full of free men like my father, who completed
his eight-year contract, and refused to sign
another.

Who will speak up for the *africanos*
by writing letters to editors in Madrid?

Someday maybe I will, but for now
all I have is this job, carrying
words that will sail
to China.

Luxurious Words

At La Casa de Lam, some of the messages I carry
are letters to editors, but most are business deals
that result in shipments of jade, silk, porcelain,
lacquer-ware, furniture, medical herbs,
ivory figurines, sandalwood incense,
and other elegant
Shanghai treasures.

None of it is enough to make me value money
more than books.

At school, I study, then at work, I run,
and later, in my quiet room at night,
I write in my diary, remembering
every detail.

The Words of Emperors

When my father visits, I overhear his conversations
with Señor Lam, about injustice on this lion-fanged
island of brutal eight-year contracts.

The emperor signed a treaty with Spain,
agreeing to provide a quarter million workers,
ordinary farmers from Canton Province,
laborers for sugar plantations in Cuba and Peru.

As soon as the indentured men arrived on this island,
they were baptized and given Catholic saints' names,
during ceremonies spoken in Latin, a language
only priests understand.

The indenture system must end, my father insists.
Absolutely, Señor Lam agrees, as they go on and on,
speaking Cantonese, while I translate their words
in my mind, practicing Spanish so that someday
I can write letters to editors
in Madrid.

Warlike Words

The next day at school, instead of writing an essay
on ancient Greek philosophy, I hand my teacher
a page scrawled with rage.
Fierce words.
Ferocious words.
Words that stab, bite, scratch,
and threaten to burst into flames.
But my peaceful teacher smiles and says I'm learning
how to fight for my future, instead of battling
the past.

Looking for another great book?
Find it
IN THE MIDDLE.

Fun, fantastic books for kids
in the in-be**TWEEN** age.

IntheMiddleBooks.com

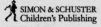

*Each time we fly back to our everyday
lives, one of my two selves
is left behind. . . .*

IN THIS HAUNTINGLY BEAUTIFUL MEMOIR,
Newbery Honor–winner Margarita Engle tells of
growing up with two cultures during a time of cold
hostility between the United States and Cuba, and
of the childhood that shaped this sensitive young
girl into an award-winning poet.

PRINT AND EBOOK EDITIONS AVAILABLE
simonandschuster.com/teen